Abie Longstaff

How to Catch a Witch

SCHOLASTIC

First published in the UK by Scholastic Ltd, 2016
Scholastic Children's Books
An imprint of Scholastic Ltd
Euston House, 24 Eversholt Street, London, NW1 1DB, UK
Registered office: Westfield Road, Southam, Warwickshire, CV47 0RA
SCHOLASTIC and associated logos are trademarks and/or
registered trademarks of Scholastic Inc.

ISBN 978 1407 16251 5

A CIP catalogue record for this book
is available from the British Library.

Printed by CPI Group (UK) Ltd, Croydon, CR0 4YY
Papers used by Scholastic Children's Books are made
from wood grown in sustainable forests.

3 5 7 9 10 8 6 4

www.scholastic.co.uk

How to
Catch
a
Witch

For K & E and for Carla

Chapter One

It's A Twister!

Charlie was dreaming.

The house was flying through the air, spinning and bumping on the wind.

She was off to Oz to see the Munchkins.

Here came Glinda, floating around in a pink bubble saying, "Charlie, Hogwarts is expecting you. Wear your blue-and-white dress."

Then she was falling.

Down...

Down...

Down...

Creak!

What was that? Charlie sat bolt upright in bed, her heart pounding.

1

The wind was howling outside. The cottage groaned and the windows rattled like a steam train. Charlie frowned. The air had a funny crackle to it – a kind of dry electricity she could almost touch. It made her think of sparks and shooting stars.

Still half asleep, she felt her way towards the window. Her hands fumbled in the dark, reaching out to emptiness. It was gone! Her window had disappeared! Then ... no, no it hadn't ... she was in the *new* house; the window was on the *left* now.

Her younger sister Annie began to cry in the room next door. Charlie opened her door on to the hallway. She rushed to her little sister but Mum was there already. "Shush now," said Mum, stroking Annie's back. "It's just the wind."

There was a loud *whoosh* from outside, and the crackle in the air grew stronger. A strange buzzing feeling ran straight up Charlie's back from her spine to her neck, making her shiver.

"Ew ... it feels so weird!" She wriggled and twisted, trying to shake off the odd sensation.

"What does?" said Mum. She picked Annie up and patted her back. "There, the storm's dying down now."

Charlie held her breath. Mum was right. The wind had stopped, and with it the funny feeling. Charlie exhaled in relief.

"What's wrong?" came her brother's voice from behind her.

"Nothing," Charlie said quickly.

"Bet you thought it was ghosts or something!" Matt cuffed her shoulder affectionately. "Like the time you thought there were goblins in the garage."

"I only said there m-m-m-*might* be. There were loads of weird noises."

"And when you thought Mr Chapman was a wizard. . ."

"Well, he had a very odd hat."

Matt shook his head and grinned at her. "Muppet," he said.

Charlie poked her tongue out at him and grinned back.

Dad popped his head around the doorway. "Right, since we're all up, I'm making pancakes," he declared. He lifted Annie from Mum and headed downstairs.

Charlie went back into her bedroom and closed the door. She pulled the heavy curtains open, letting the weak morning light creep into the room. Charlie sat on her window seat and watched the last of the wind pulling on the branches of the trees. She was still trying to shake the unsettled feeling it had given her. That buzzing was really odd! Although, she had to admit, Matt had a point: everywhere she went, Charlie noticed strange things. There was that frog the other day who had looked at her closely, like he was about to talk. And the old apple tree at the bottom of the garden definitely had some kind of face in its bark. These days things had seemed stranger than ever. They'd only moved into the cottage one week earlier and so far it was all very different from London. She pulled out her notebook and found the list entitled "Strange Things".

1) Old man with the beard. (Is he some kind of soothsayer?)
2) Small child with ~~big~~ massive eyes.
3) Three black cats (esp. the one that glared at me).
4) Wiggly old apple tree with a face like a troll.
5) Frogs croaking in rhyme (v. odd).
6) Enormous pumpkin. (Do they really grow that big? Sign of enchantment?)

She added:

7) Strange buzzing.

Then she closed her notebook and looked at her watch. Seven-thirty a.m. Twenty-five hours until she started at her new school. Charlie gulped. She felt sick at the thought of it. It was horrible going into Year Seven right in the middle of Easter term. Everyone would already know each other. She was going to be the only new person. Charlie turned a page and started to make a list of things to pack before tomorrow.

"Charlie!" Dad called from downstairs, "Can you go to the shops and buy eggs?" Classic Dad. He'd obviously got halfway through pancake-making before realizing they didn't have all the ingredients.

"What about Matt? Can't he g-go?" Charlie shouted back.

"I'm studying!" Matt yelled. This was plainly a lie; Charlie could hear the thump of music coming from his room.

She sighed and headed down the rickety cottage stairs. Each step was so teeny it was like it had been built by elves. Charlie touched the wall for support. The second her fingertips met the old stone wall, she felt the strange buzzing sensation again, but stronger this time, like an itching right in the middle of her bones. She took her hand off the wall and shook her head to clear it. This

cottage was creepy. It definitely should go on the Strange
Things list:

8) Creepy cottage (possibly haunted?)

From the first moment Charlie had set foot in the
doorway she'd felt there was something odd about it.
What was it? Ghosts? A poltergeist? A vampire living
in the cellar? Well, whatever it was, there was no way
Charlie was going to mention it – she'd be giving Matt
enough ammunition to tease her for years!

"Go away," Charlie whispered, just in case the ghost-
vampire thing was listening.

Downstairs, the kitchen was a mess. Dad was
planning to build everything himself, from scratch. It
would save money, he said. So until then, there were
piles of wood lying across the floor, the fridge was
precariously balanced on a stack of floor tiles waiting to
be laid, and the microwave had to be pulled out from
behind a mountain of worktops Dad had bought on
eBay.

Charlie climbed over a heap of boxes to find Dad
standing by the grimy old hob covered in flour. Annie
was patting his shoulder, giggling as she made clouds
appear.

"Thanks, Charlie," said Dad, handing her a pound coin. "Don't go to the deli – it's too expensive. Go to the supermarket."

"But that's all the way at the other end!"

"I know, but—"

"Yeah, yeah. It'll save *money*."

"Yep!" Dad gave an overly cheery smile.

Charlie pocketed the coin and pulled on her shoes.

"Bye!" she yelled as she closed the door. It shook on the hinges as it slammed and Charlie sighed. The cottage was falling to pieces! It was a miracle, really, that the wind hadn't blown it all the way over that morning. No one had done anything to it for years, the lawyers had said. Not since Great-Aunt Bess had died. Dad was going to be very busy.

Charlie turned and headed down the tangled garden path and along the lane to the village. It was so quiet now the wind was still. She could hear the slap of her shoes on the ground as she walked.

Caw!

Charlie jumped. A big bird with black feathers stared down at her from the apple tree. It looked like some kind of crow. It cocked its head to the side, as if it was assessing her. Then it gave a little nod, and flew off. To her list, Charlie mentally added:

9) Spooky crow.

She headed into the village, past the Spindle pub and the Washer Woman Laundrette. It was all so twee here: cobbled streets and little shops selling sweets and cakes. There was even a bunting-covered bandstand where local group the Three Minstrels played. Mum said it was one of the oldest villages in England and they were really lucky to live in such a special place. Charlie didn't share her enthusiasm. Just because Mum had inherited a creepy house in the middle of nowhere didn't mean they had to actually *live* in it.

Charlie reached the supermarket and walked through the shiny automatic doors in relief. At least something looked like the city here. She fingered the familiar packaging as she passed along the aisles. Eggs. She looked around till she spotted them. Her eyes scanned the prices and she immediately ruled out *Golden Goose: Luxury Eggs for the Discerning Shopper* and picked up *Basic Range*.

Coming out of the supermarket she turned right and walked on. It took her a second to realize she'd taken the wrong road. The sign read WOOD STREET, and it looked like this road ran parallel to the high street. She was about to turn back when, from an open window ahead, came the sound of singing. Whoever it was could really sing.

Curious, Charlie stepped towards the noise. Before her stood a castle. She looked closer. No, it wasn't a real castle. Someone had just added stone turrets to the roof. There was a big iron gate and a sign that read CASTLE HOUSE.

Something touched her leg. Charlie jumped and dropped the eggs, which smashed on the ground. She looked down, and immediately felt stupid. A small black cat glared up at her, stepped gingerly over the mess of eggs and sticky cardboard, and walked off. Charlie bent down to see if any of the eggs could be saved.

"Oh my goodness!" came a soft voice from the open window above her. "Wait there!"

Charlie looked up but the speaker had gone in a swish of blonde hair.

Moments later the front door opened and a girl came rushing out. The sun was in Charlie's eyes, so the first thing she saw was the shiny outline of a person with a halo of sparkle around her head. She looked like a princess.

"I am sooo sorry! Naughty Boots!" The princess shook a finger at the cat's retreating tail. Then she reached out and gave Charlie a box of Golden Goose eggs. "Please, take these!" she said earnestly.

"No, n-n-no," Charlie stammered.

"Please!" the princess repeated and she held the carton out insistently.

"Th-th-thanks," Charlie answered, her fingers fumbling to take the box. She couldn't stop staring at the girl. There was something completely mesmerizing about her. Her hair was all swooshy and shiny, like in a shampoo ad, and her bright blue eyes were sparkling in the sunlight. She smiled at Charlie warmly.

"I'm Suzy." She held out her hand delicately for Charlie to shake. As their fingers touched Charlie felt the buzzing run through her body, like a low-level electric shock. She jumped back, holding tightly on to the eggs so she didn't drop another carton. The second she moved away, the feeling stopped.

Suzy didn't blink. It was like she hadn't noticed anything strange. She smiled again and gave a little wave. "Nice to meet you!" she sang, and then pivoted on the tips of her shoes, picked up the cat, and danced back into the castle.

"That definitely counts as number 10," Charlie muttered to herself.

Number 11 came later that evening. Charlie was

searching for her pencil case. It was supposed to be in one of the boxes marked CHARLIE'S STUFF, but instead it seemed to have vanished into thin air. She turned a small packing box upside down, emptied it into the bottom of her wardrobe, and sifted through. Nope. But, ah – there were her PE trainers. Good.

The doorbell went.

"Someone get that!" Mum called. "I'm reading Annie a story."

"I'm in the bath!" Dad yelled.

"I'm still studying!" Matt shouted. (Another lie.)

Charlie stomped downstairs and opened the front door. On the doorstep was an old lady dressed in bright orange, with an orange hat, orange hair, an orange dress and orange shoes.

"Would you like to buy some dishcloths?" she asked in a gravelly voice.

Charlie put her hand to her throat in sympathy, then quickly took it back in case the woman thought she was making fun of her. "Er, no, th-thanks," she answered.

"Really?" the lady pressed. "Everyone buys dishcloths from me. They say mine are the best in the land."

"The b-best in the land?" Charlie repeated.

"Oh, yes."

"Um, thanks but I th-think we're fine."

The lady's eyes narrowed. "You might regret it," she croaked.

"What do you m-mean?" Charlie asked nervously.

"Well, it's two for one today." The lady gave a broad smile. "I'll come and see you next month. Perhaps you might need dishcloths then? Yes?"

"Um. . . OK." Charlie closed the door.

Yep. Number 11 on the Strange Things list. Charlie grimaced. *Or . . . maybe it's me that's the strange one.* No one else had noticed anything odd. She sighed. *I'm just nervous about the new school, that's all. Once tomorrow is over, then everything will feel much better.* She made her way back up the tiny stairs, taking extra care not to touch the old stone wall on the way.

Chapter Two

Lions and Tigers and Bears! Oh My!

"Charlie! Up! Up now! We overslept!" Mum was in a panic, running down the corridor and into Annie's room to get her dressed.

"Urgh," Charlie mumbled. Her head was thick and woolly, and she felt like she'd only just got to sleep.

Then, all at once, her brain kicked into gear and she jumped up. New school. Her stomach dropped and she began to dress as quickly as she could, her hands shaking and fumbling over the shirt buttons.

Charlie could hear Mum shouting at Matt to get up too as she hopped back past the doorway, pulling her nurse's uniform over her head. Attached to her hip was a wriggling Annie, yelling, "Down! Down! Want get down!"

Charlie made her way to the kitchen. She picked her way across a stack of table legs and sat on a box marked OVEN.

As Mum continued to yell upstairs, Dad clambered over the table legs towards Charlie. He took a long look around the kitchen. "This is a *biiig* project," he said slowly. He bit his bottom lip and sighed through his teeth.

Charlie looked at him in sympathy as she nibbled a piece of bread.

Dad patted his new library book: *Restoring Your 17th Century Home.* "I guess it's lucky I haven't got a job to do as well," he said with a wry grin.

Since he'd been made redundant six months ago, Dad had gone for interview after interview, trying to find a new job. But no one wanted to hire him. Apparently he was too good, so that made him too expensive. It didn't really make sense to Charlie. All she knew was that heavy feeling at the base of her tummy when he came home from yet another failed interview.

Now he was running his hands through his curly hair, working out the distance from one wall to the other. Charlie felt a rush of affection. "The k-k—" she started to say, but to her surprise she got stuck on the "K" and the "kitchen" wouldn't come out. She shook her head, hurrying to change her sentence before Dad noticed and started fussing. Quickly she said, "It's going to be lovely."

Too late. Dad had raised his eyebrows. "You OK, love?" he said.

Charlie nodded.

"Ah. School's going to be fine. Don't worry so much!" He grinned and ruffled her hair.

Charlie smiled weakly. Inside her stomach was churning. Was her stutter worse today? While Dad's back was turned she practised "k, k, k, k" under her breath.

Matt was the next to climb through the obstacle course. "Morning!" He jumped over the table legs and scooped up the peanut butter jar, flicking it from hand to hand. "Hey, Charlie! Here's to our first day!" he said, saluting her with the jar.

"Nervous?" Charlie asked.

"Nah. We'll be fine."

Charlie screwed up her face. Yeah right.

On the drive to school Charlie looked out of the window and tried to get her bearings. Mum would be dropping them off every morning, but in the afternoons, Charlie would have to walk home on her own.

"Here we are!" sang Mum. Charlie felt her tummy collapse as she pulled open the car door. "Good luck! Smile! Be nice! See you later!" Mum waved as she sped off to take Annie to nursery.

Charlie turned to Matt, but he'd gone, rushing straight for the school office as if he couldn't wait to meet a whole load of new people. She took a deep breath, squared her shoulders, and began to walk down the gravel driveway, closing her fists tight and trying to concentrate on looking normal.

Two seconds later, she'd tripped over her shoelace and landed on her knees in a puddle.

There was a snigger, and Charlie looked up to see a group of boys laughing. Red-faced, she scrambled to her feet and gathered the contents of her school bag as quickly as she could.

"Oh!" came a soft voice, and there was a patter of footsteps as someone rushed to help her.

Charlie turned and blushed even more. It was Suzy, the princess from yesterday. She bounced towards Charlie, her pretty face creased in a delicate frown.

"Poor you!" She crouched down, swiftly gathered Charlie's belongings into a neat pile and brushed off the dust. This time Charlie was careful not to touch Suzy's hands as she took her books back.

16

Suzy gave a beautiful smile. "See you!" she said, and she danced on into school.

"Th-thanks," Charlie mumbled to her retreating back.

She pulled herself up and tried to hold her head high as she continued down the path, past the boys, and through the front door into Broomwood School.

Chapter
Three

Guess My Name

"Hey, there you are," said Matt. He turned back to speak into a hatch cut out of glass. "This is my sister, Charlotte."

"Charlotte Samuels. Year Seven?" the woman behind the desk asked.

Charlie nodded.

Matt nudged her. "Answer her, then."

Charlie blushed. "Y-yes," she managed.

"Right – if you both wait on the sofa, a buddy from your year will come to collect you."

They sat, swinging their feet, and before long a boy came. "Matt? Year Nine?" he said.

"Hey," Matt drawled.

"Hi, I'm Tom," the boy answered.

"Hey, Tom. Cool cuffs. Love those leather ones."

"Yeah. I bought them at the market. . ."

Charlie watched as Matt set off down the corridor with his first friend. How easy he made it look!

"Good luck!" called Matt over his shoulder. "Smile! Be nice!" Charlie couldn't help laughing at his wicked impression of Mum. She looked around self-consciously in case anyone had heard her, but the corridor had emptied.

Charlie sat there, twisting her fingers, lacing them into each other and out again. It was beginning to feel like everyone had forgotten her. Finally a tall girl with spiky hair rushed in. "Charlotte? Year Seven?" she said quickly.

Charlie nodded.

"Everyone else was busy so I was sent to collect you," Spiky said in a cross tone. "I'm in Year Twelve," she added airily, "But I'll show you around anyway."

"Hi." Charlie gave her a wobbly smile.

"OK. So, this is the office" – Spiky began walking quickly along the corridor – "the library" – she waved vaguely with her left hand – "the canteen, the girls' loos, the art room is up there" – she pointed to some steps – "and the hall is down there. OK?"

Charlie nodded again and tried to look as if she was remembering everything.

"OK, so, um . . . all the normal rules: don't run in the corridor, you can't stay in the classrooms over lunch, Years Twelve and Thirteen get the tables by the window in the canteen, and you can't go into the common room either – that's just for us."

Charlie glanced down the hall and quickly dropped her gaze. Suzy was standing outside the common room with a group of girls around her.

Charlie lifted her eyes carefully and tried to stop herself staring. Suzy was in school uniform, like everyone else, but where other kids looked scruffy and crumpled, she was elegant and polished. Her honey-coloured hair was neatly swept back in two glittered clips and even her nails were painted a baby pink. Charlie looked at her own hands. The nails were bitten down to the quick, and on her wrist her chewed friendship bracelet was ragged and grubby at the edges. Her skirt had twisted and was now back to front, with her shirt sticking out of one side. She hastily swung it back round and began to smooth her crazy curls.

"That's Suzy Evans," said Spiky in a tone of great reverence. "She's in my year. We're both in the school show," she added proudly. "I'm a flying monkey and Suzy's Dorothy, but we've got loads of scenes together." She paused for a moment. "So I'll leave you here, yeah?

Your form room is just back by the library. You've got Miss Robbins. She'll teach you English too."

Charlie nodded vigorously and looked at her timetable. English was first thing.

"I've got to get back to my friends now," said Spiky. "You know, Suzy and people. Oh," she looked down at Charlie's feet, "here's a tip – no one wears white socks. I know it's the school uniform but everyone wears grey." She waved her hand. "See you!"

Charlie glanced at her socks. When she lifted her head a split second later, Spiky had disappeared.

Charlie walked back the way they'd come and tried to remember where the library was. Finally she found it and, next door, her classroom. There was a teacher's voice coming from behind the door. Charlie took a deep breath and lifted her fist to knock. The voice stopped then said, "Come in."

With her stomach churning, Charlie pushed the door open. A sea of faces looked up.

"Um. . . I'm, uh. . ." She stumbled over her first words. Everyone stared. The teacher waited, expectantly. Charlie opened her mouth but, to her horror, she found she couldn't say the "ch" of her name.

There was a long pause. Charlie could hear her name inside her head but it was like the sounds were stuck in quicksand: the more she tried to pull them out, the deeper they sank. She tried the "ch", "ch" for Charlotte. She screwed up her face, willing the word to come. There was a giggle from the back of the class.

"Rumpelstiltskin!" a boy shouted and everyone laughed.

Charlie's cheeks were growing hot and she could feel tears prickling in her eyes. In desperation, she tried her surname: "SSSSamuels," she burst out, a little too loudly.

Realization hit the teacher. "Oh," Miss Robbins said as she shuffled through the pieces of paper on her desk. "I have a Charlotte on my list," she said slowly, as if Charlie was stupid. "Is that you?"

Charlie nodded miserably.

"Good. Well, take a seat. Next to Sara." She waved her hand in Sara's direction.

Sara stared for a brief second, then said, "Oh, Miss, Nicola sits here, remember? She's at the doctor this morning." She hastily covered the empty desk with her arms.

"Right." The teacher looked around impatiently, and then pointed to a desk on its own. "Just sit there for now. We'll find somewhere proper for you later."

The chair scraped noisily as Charlie pulled it out.

"Back to work, everyone . . . concentrating please. . ."

Miss Robbins clapped her hands. "Charlotte, you've joined us halfway through a project so you'll have to work hard to catch up."

Charlie nodded and stared at the handout Miss Robbins had given her.

The Brothers Grimm.

Below that, the words swam about in her wet eyes. She blinked to clear them. Stupid voice! Stupid words. "Ch," she whispered softly to herself. There. She *could* do it. What was wrong with her today? Her stutter hadn't been this bad since she was little. She closed her eyes and tried to listen to Miss Robbins.

"The fairy tales you know today are very different to the tales documented by the Brothers Grimm. The tales of their time were frightening, heavy with morals, often about death. Some were distorted versions of true events, told as a warning. I'm going to tell you a story behind a fairy tale. See if you recognize the tale it became. . ."

Charlie breathed in and out slowly. She could feel eyes staring into her back. Not only was she the new girl, she was the new girl with the stammer.

". . .it's the story of a woman named Katharina, a famous baker in the seventeenth century. A man called Hans was jealous of her ability, and, desperate to learn the recipe for her popular gingerbread, he proposed to her, but she refused him. To escape Hans, Katharina moved to a cottage in the forest and continued her baking. Hans denounced the baker as a witch. She was brought before the court, but no evidence of witchcraft could be found, so Katharina was set free. Hans and his sister Grete tracked down Katharina's cottage in the woods. In their fury, they killed the baker and threw her into her baking oven."

Charlie knew the story was "Hansel and Gretel", but there was no way she was risking her voice again. She kept her head down all morning and let her hair hang over her face like a curtain.

At the lunch bell everyone rushed up out of their seats and the room was filled with people chatting and laughing in little groups. Charlie couldn't bear to stand up and walk through them all, so she sat at her desk, fiddling with her hair and sneaking little looks around. The girls seemed very giggly. Spiky was right – they were all wearing grey socks, not white. No one was wearing a friendship bracelet either. Charlie pushed hers under her shirt cuff. She'd made it with her old friends, but here, in her new life, it suddenly looked out of place and babyish.

The rest of the day passed in a blur. Occasionally

Charlie saw the back of her brother's head drift past, in a throng of thirteen-year-old boys. She shook her head, marvelling at Matt's ability to make friends wherever he went. Charlie pulled her hair over her face and tried to look like she didn't mind being by herself.

That night the family ate dinner while sitting on the kitchen chairs with plates balanced on their knees. Charlie played with her food as Matt told Mum and Dad about Broomwood.

"It's so great!" he said. "Everyone's really friendly. Can I have Felix over next week? He's really into spray-painting, and he said he'd show me how he makes T-shirts and stuff."

"Sure," said Mum. "What about you, Charlie? How are you doing?"

"Mmm," Charlie nodded. "Fine."

"That's good!" said Mum. She sounded relieved. Charlie looked down.

"Ugh! This bacon is chewy," said Matt. He lifted a long string of rind.

"It's not brilliant," Dad admitted, "but it was on offer!" he added proudly.

"Hey, Charlie," Mum changed the subject really unsubtly, "how are you getting on with your room? Have

26

you unpacked those boxes yet?"

"Not yet," Charlie answered. "I'm g-g... I will, though." Mum looked at Dad again.

Great. Now she'd added another worry to Mum and Dad's list. Charlie clenched her teeth together and willed her voice to work better tomorrow.

Chapter Four

Something Wicked This Way Comes

Tuesday was bad.

Wednesday was worse.

By Thursday Charlie felt like her throat had completely closed. She couldn't understand it. She'd always had a stammer and, yes, there had been periods where it had been really bad, but not like this. It felt like her words were at the bottom of a deep well and every sentence meant hauling them up, heavy and dripping with sludge.

On Thursday morning Charlie had maths. Mr Wyatt was picking on people to answer questions. *Please not me, please not me,* went the voice in Charlie's head.

But sure enough, Mr Wyatt pointed straight at her. "Charlotte?"

Charlie knew the answer was *cosine*. But she could feel her skin prickling and her palms sweating at the thought of speaking out loud. *Please,* she told her body silently, *please don't stammer again, not in front of everyone. Please don't let me down.* But something about the "C" was locked away, deep at the bottom of the well. She ran through letters in her head. She could manage a "T", her tongue decided. So, rather than risk humiliation by stuttering all over the place, Charlie said, "Tangent."

"No, no," said Mr Wyatt, disappointed. "Anyone else?"

Charlie had taken to hiding in the library every break time so she didn't have to talk to anyone. As she passed people in the corridor, she tried not to make eye contact. She pulled up her hood and yanked her long curls across her face. She got in the habit of following people wherever they were going, so she didn't have to ask anyone the way. Mostly this worked and she made it to lessons by letting the flow of people-traffic lead her along – until Thursday lunch, when, without thinking, she followed a group of girls straight into the hall.

A large group was gathered around the piano by the stage and a teacher was calling out, "Who's next?"

Charlie backed away hastily into the doorway.

A girl bounced on to the stage. "Me, Miss Knevitt."

"Ah, Suzy!" The teacher's voice softened. "Let's hear your best 'Somewhere Over the Rainbow'."

Charlie held her breath as Suzy Evans lifted her head and began to sing. Her voice was perfect, soulful. It made tingles run along Charlie's spine.

"Magic," breathed Miss Knevitt as Suzy reached the top notes.

Then, abruptly, Suzy made a funny face and a strange noise came out of her throat. It sounded like a loud croaaaakk. Suzy went bright red and clapped her hand over her mouth.

The audience giggled and Miss Knevitt shuffled her music papers. "I think we'll leave it there, dear," she said. "Don't want you straining your voice."

Suzy looked down, mortified.

Charlie fidgeted. There was that weird crackle in the air again. She wriggled her shoulders up and down to shake it off. She lifted her head and saw a girl watching her. The girl was sitting on a chair at the side of the hall with her legs tucked under her, Buddha-style, and her socks were neon-yellow with green stripes, brazenly flaunting the school rules. She wore enormous glasses that were balanced precariously on her tiny face, and her red hair was cut short. She looked like a little pixie playing dress-up. There was a funny expression on her freckly face, like she was squinting. As she stared at Charlie, she screwed up her eyes even further.

Charlie backed away and rushed to the library. She breathed out slowly. Poor Suzy. How embarrassing! She winced in sympathy. And why was that glasses girl looking at Charlie so strangely? Charlie stayed hidden between the aisles until the bell went.

After school Charlie played with Annie while Dad made dinner. Dad had been to London yesterday about a job opportunity. From the sounds of things, it hadn't gone well. She could hear him crashing and bashing the pots in the kitchen as he moved in-between the packing boxes.

She set up the wooden train track for Annie and whizzed Thomas the Tank Engine over the bridges and into the tunnels again and again.

"Story, Charlie?" Annie said hopefully.

So they lay on the cushions by the sofa and Charlie read her "The Little Mermaid" from *The Big Book of Fairy Tales*, Annie's current favourite. Somehow, even though she couldn't trust her voice at school, it felt stronger when she read to Annie. Annie loved all the different accents and she liked Charlie's scary witch cackle best of all. "Wa-hah-hah-hah!" They shouted it together. It felt wonderful to be talking again. She made a wicked witch face and Annie grinned back.

"Hey! I'm home!" called Mum. She walked through the front door and flung herself down on the sofa, kicking off her shoes.

"Wa-hah-hah!" cackled Annie as she climbed up to join her.

"Oof!" Mum yelped as Annie landed on her tummy. She leaned sideways to Charlie and took her hand. "How are you getting on, love?" she asked.

"OK," Charlie shrugged.

"Have you made any friends yet?"

Charlie squirmed. "Not yet," she said. Mum frowned. "But I'm sure I will s-s-s-soon," she added hastily.

"What about your old friends? Have you called Claire and Amira?"

"No . . . I just want to settle in here f-f-first."

Mum nodded.

"Dinner in twenty!" yelled Dad from the kitchen. "Dawn, can you put Annie to bed? She's already eaten."

"Come on, sleepy-pie." Mum picked Annie up, and Charlie waved goodnight.

It wasn't true, what she'd said to Mum. The real reason she hadn't called Claire and Amira was because she hadn't heard from them in ages. They were busy. Charlie had seen their Facebook photos. Busy at Charlie's old school, in her old street, with her old group, and Charlie didn't want to hear about it. Tears prickled the back of her eyes and, not for the first time, she cursed Dad's old boss for making them move. This time last year she didn't even know what the word "redundancy" meant. She'd been going about her life, her days of stuttering long gone, and she had been happy.

Everyone was quiet at dinner. Charlie couldn't trust herself to start a conversation. The last thing she wanted was for Mum and Dad to start fussing about her stammer. Mum looked exhausted. Dad was scowling at his food. Even Matt didn't say much.

The kitchen was full of boxes, so they all sat in the lounge on a sofa covered in old cloth, balancing their plates on their knees again. Dad was halfway through painting, and there were bits of sandpaper, rags, pots of paint and brushes on every surface available. The whole room stank of white spirit. Charlie tried not to breathe too deeply.

Mum put down her fork and sighed loudly. Dad transferred his plate to his left knee so he could lean over and put his hand over hers. "Hang in there, love," he murmured.

"I'm OK." Mum put on her cheery voice. "I'm just getting used to full-time work, that's all. I'd forgotten how physical nursing is!" She gave a little laugh. "It'll be fine soon. I'm just tired."

After dinner Charlie carried the plates into the messy kitchen. She could hear Mum and Dad murmuring in the lounge. Their voices were quiet, but Charlie knew what they were saying. It had been the same for the last few months. What would they do if Dad couldn't find a job? Charlie knew Mum's nursing salary wasn't high.

Matt looked at her as they did the washing up, but neither of them said anything. They just listened to the murmur, murmur, murmur of worries drifting through the house.

Chapter Five

Well Met

Early in the morning Charlie had another odd dream. She was in the cottage, but it was long ago. There were candles placed in all the alcoves and she could hear a funny kind of chanting voice coming from somewhere down in the cellar.

Miss Robbins was outside, saying, "Push her in the oven, Gretel!" and the weird orange dishcloth lady kept repeating:

"You'll regret it! You'll regret it! I'll take your voice, Little Mermaid!"

Charlie woke up, all confused. She moved her jaw from side to side and practised her old voice exercises. "La, la, la," she sang quietly into the darkness.

She kept thinking of that strange peddler woman

with the dishcloths. Maybe she'd put a curse on Charlie. Charlie shook her head – now she was being really silly! She reached for her notebook and made a list of logical reasons her stammer was worse:

1) Just started new school
2) Don't know anyone
3) Strange cottage
4) Weird buzzy feeling
5) Normal to have phases of stammer being worse
6) Worrying about it too much

She chewed the end of her pen and, before she knew it, she'd added:

7) Cursed by peddler

Then she crossed it out again, feeling like an idiot. *I just need a break from the weird cottage and everything*, she told herself. After school she would go into the village and have a walk around. Then she'd see that everything was totally normal and there was nothing strange going on at all.

*

After the last lesson, Charlie went straight to her locker to put her books away. The corridor was filled with people laughing and chatting, saying goodbyes and making plans to meet up or text each other. Charlie played with her things in her locker, trying to pretend she didn't mind that no one was talking to her.

She closed the locker door and turned to see Pixie Glasses Girl standing across the hall. The girl was squinting again, this time at Suzy Evans, who was walking towards them, waving goodbye to friends as she went. Everyone in the corridor watched as Suzy walked by, hoping to earn a wave or a nod. To Charlie's amazement, Suzy smiled directly at her:

"See you tomorrow!" she sang out.

Charlie felt a jolt of current. The second Suzy passed her it was gone. Charlie looked up and caught the eye of Glasses Girl across the corridor, and saw her own puzzled expression mirrored on the girl's face. Glasses took a step towards Charlie, then...

"Watch out, Kat!" Spiky brushed by, rushing to catch up with Suzy, and knocking Glasses backwards as she went. Glasses mumbled something and turned down a side corridor.

Charlie pulled her rucksack on to her back and walked out of school towards home, deep in thought.

Kat. Glasses Girl was called Kat. She didn't have any lessons with Charlie so she must be in another year group. Had Kat felt the crackle in the air too? Was that why she was frowning? Charlie couldn't tell. Even if she didn't have a stutter there was no way Charlie would risk asking her. She'd look like some kind of loony!

Charlie turned right past the supermarket and on to the high street. It was good to be out. She breathed in deeply. London had been a big mix of fumes and tarmac and chip shops and curry houses. It smelled so different here: of horses and cut grass and sharp wind. It was so fresh she could pick each scent out.

Wait. Something smelled amazing. *Mmm, bakery smells.* Pastry and sugars and caramels.

She felt in her bag and found a pound. She looked at it guiltily. It was supposed to be for emergencies, Mum had said. A jam tart wasn't *exactly* an emergency. Charlie forced herself to turn away.

Next to the bakery was a little shop Charlie hadn't seen before. It was a black-and-white Tudor kind of building, with wonky beams and a crumbling roof. It was called "Moonquest" and had lots of crystals and dreamcatchers hanging in the window. Without thinking, Charlie pushed the door and went in.

A little bell jangled and a man with a long ponytail

looked up. "Hey there," he said, and looked down again.

Charlie wandered around the shelves looking at little stone animals, and pendants, and incense burners. There was a pile of brown fabric bags that smelled funny. Charlie read their labels:

MONEY DRAWING

FAST LUCK

CAST OFF EVIL

COURAGE

They were spells! Before she could stop herself, Charlie scanned the bags for one that read SPEAKING or CLEAR VOICE, but there was nothing.

"You all right there?" Ponytail asked. "Are you looking for something?"

Charlie shook her head quickly, waved goodbye and hurried out to avoid having to speak.

As she headed on down the street her mind was filled with the thought of a spell – a spell to stop her stammer. That would be so cool! Imagine being able to swallow something that made her voice loud and clear: something to get rid of whatever was blocking her. Charlie stopped walking. There was that spell called CAST OFF EVIL. What if she did have a curse on her? What if that spell could lift it?

No. No. That kind of thing never worked. It was just

bits of grass and herbs in hessian. It wasn't a proper spell – not like something a witch would make. Charlie grinned as she pictured a green-skinned old hag pouring smoking potions into a big cauldron, reciting a recipe. Now *that* really would be great!

A flashback hit her all in a rush. Last night she'd dreamed of the sound of chanting from the cellar! She gave a little shiver. She was so wrapped up in her thoughts she nearly bumped straight into a low wall. Looking up, her eyes registered white stone and a wooden plaque:

BROOMWOOD WISHING WELL IS RUMOURED
TO BE THE OLDEST IN ENGLAND.
PEOPLE HAVE WISHED ON ITS WATERS
FOR HUNDREDS OF YEARS.

The wishing well was cute. It had a little grey roof, like a pointed witch's hat. Charlie sat on the edge, staring down into the blackness below. She leaned in and whispered:

"I need a witch!"

Then she sat up and giggled.

It was only later that she realized she'd said the whole phrase without stammering even once.

*

By the time she got home Charlie was in a much better mood.

Dad was sawing in the garden. "Mind holding the end for me, love?" he said as he wiped his forehead.

"Sure. Wh-what are you m-mak-k-k. . . designing?"

"It's going to be the worktop in the kitchen. . . Thanks. That's done now." Dad whistled merrily as he added the long board to a pile on the porch. Charlie smiled at him. DIY was obviously a good distraction from failed interviews!

She climbed over his toolbox and went upstairs to do her homework. For English, Miss Robbins wanted them to do some research into storybook witches and their powers. Charlie ruled out her lines neatly and began to write. Before long she had:

Story	Witch ability
The Little Mermaid	Turning tails into legs; Removing voice
Snow White	Disguise; Making poison apple

Rapunzel	Imprisoning young girls
Beauty and the Beast	Turning prince into beast
Hansel and Gretel	Making a gingerbread cottage
Sleeping Beauty	Making girl sleep for a hundred years
The Wizard of Oz	Enslaving beasts eg. flying monkeys
The Lion the Witch and the Wardrobe	Turning all seasons into winter

She put down the pen and read through her list.

Her eyes drifted down the column of powers. They were pretty impressive! Charlie thought back to what Miss Robbins had said in class. In the olden days, so-called witches were often wise women who were good with herbs and plants, medicine women of a kind. They might not have had magic wands but they had their own style of "magic": potions and tinctures and charms.

Were the witches in fairy tales just wise women, then? Actions like disguising themselves, or making poison apples could be achieved without proper magic. It was also possible that, as with Hansel and Gretel, the original stories had been distorted or exaggerated over the years.

Maybe an olden-day wise woman would have had something to help someone like Charlie: a drink or something?

Essence of clear voice, she doodled on a bit of paper.

Or ... or maybe magical witches really existed – proper witches, with proper magic potions? Witches who could transform mermaids into humans or princes into beasts? It was possible, wasn't it? Witches who could swoop in on a broomstick and magic her stammer away ... all Charlie had to do was catch one as she flew by.

Charlie copied the table into her notebook, this time adding another column:

Witch locations

Story	Witch Locations	Witch ability
The Little Mermaid	Underwater cave	Turning tails into legs; Removing voice

Snow White	Palace (stepmother)	Disguise; Making poison apple
Rapunzel	Radish patch	Imprisoning young girls
Beauty and the Beast	Arrives on prince's doorstep	Turning prince into beast
Hansel and Gretel	Woods	Making a gingerbread cottage
Sleeping Beauty	Turns up at Christening	Making girl sleep for a hundred years
The Six Swans	Palace (stepmother)	Turning boys into swans
The Wizard of Oz	Munchkinland	Enslaving beasts eg. flying monkeys
The Lion the Witch and the Wardrobe	Narnia	Turning all seasons into winter

Charlie looked through the list. Witches always seemed to crop up in situations that were nothing like hers. She didn't rate her chances of finding an underwater cave. Nor was she likely to end up in Munchkinland as tornados weren't exactly common in the village. Maybe she could wait for the next Halloween and construct a giant net?

I need a witch, she wrote and she drew little cobwebs in the *es*.

Then she shook her head. "I'm crazy!" she whispered to herself. Of course she couldn't catch a witch! She laughed. *Yep,* she told herself, *any moment now I'll be carted off to the loony bin and Mum and Dad will have to visit me every second Sunday.*

She screwed up the paper and was about to throw it in the bin when she stopped herself. If Matt found it he'd tease her for the rest of her life. She rummaged in the drawer for a match, put the screwed-up page in her fireplace, then lit the match and watched the paper burn and burn until there was nothing left – just a pile of ashes.

Chapter Six

Come Out, Come Out, Wherever You Are. . .

By the time Charlie made it downstairs the next morning Dad had already gone out to the DIY store and Mum was playing jigsaws on the lounge floor with Annie.

Charlie made herself some toast and sat on the sofa crunching it. "Where's Matt?" she asked in-between bites.

"Doing his science project."

"Really?"

"He's got a lot to do," said Mum.

"Story!" Annie interrupted, holding up *The Big Book of Fairy Tales*.

"OK. Ch-ch. . ." Charlie changed "Choose one" to "Which one do you want?"

Mum heaved herself up and stroked Charlie's head. "Thanks, love," she said softly. "I'm just going to jump in the shower."

"You OK, Mum?"

"Yep," she called over her shoulder, "just could do with a bit more sleep. If you see an old lady with a spindle, tell her I'm perfectly happy to prick my finger and nod off for a hundred years."

Annie turned the pages until she found "Hansel and Gretel". Charlie paused. This was the one Miss Robbins had said was based on a true story. While she read it out to Annie, her brain ticked over. *A true story. . .*

When Mum came back down Charlie turned on the computer and, on a whim, typed in "Snow+white+ true+story". She clicked on a link promising "the true story of Snow White" and found a website all about Countess Margarete Von Waldeck. The beautiful Countess grew up in a town where small children known as dwarfs worked underground in the mines. Margarete had a stepmother who hated her, and had died at the age of twenty-one after a mysterious poisoning. Charlie's eyes widened. She took out her notebook and looked at yesterday's table. Before she knew what she was doing, she had turned the page and begun to write:

*

Ways to Catch a Witch

1) Buy giant net

Charlie doodled designs in her notebook. Could she attach the net to some kind of sturdy stick and hang it out of her window? Then all she'd have to do was wait for Halloween and a witch would fly right in! Only ... Charlie sighed. Halloween was <u>months</u> away. She crossed out 1) and moved onto 2).

2) Get a stepmother (see <u>Snow White</u>)

Mum and Dad didn't argue very often. And, despite all the recent money trouble, they were still together, so it didn't seem likely to Charlie that she would be getting a stepmother any time soon, which was a good thing, really. She put a line through this one and scribbled:

3) Go to Narnia (see <u>The Lion The Witch and The Wardrobe</u>)

Feeling a bit stupid, Charlie made her way upstairs and cautiously pulled open her wardrobe door. At once she was nearly assaulted by falling tennis rackets, welly boots, boxes of letters, winter coats, stuffed toys and shoes that no longer fit. Checking for Narnia would mean clearing it all out. She shoved the door closed with her back, and shook her head. The whole thing was ridiculous. Of course there wasn't a magic land behind her old anorak. She turned back to her list.

4) Find a radish patch (see Rapunzel)

Charlie paused. She didn't know where to find a radish patch. She wasn't even sure what radishes looked like when they were in the ground. She put a question mark beside it and chewed her pencil for a bit.

5) Go to a christening (see Sleeping Beauty)

Charlie wracked her brains, but she couldn't think of a single baby they knew who might be being christened in the next week or so.

6) Gingerbread Cottage (see Hansel and Gretel)

Where on earth could you hide a house made of

sweets? Charlie frowned. In the story the house had been in the woods. Maybe it was worth having a wander, just on the off-chance there was a gingerbread house at the end of the garden. Charlie grinned at her own craziness. Then she shrugged. Well, why not? It gave her something to do.

She looked out of the window – argh … it was already dark. Fine. Charlie closed her book. She'd go first thing tomorrow.

After breakfast, Charlie packed her notebook in a rucksack and set off.

She walked down to the end of the garden and climbed over the stone wall. The cottage garden backed on to woods. It was one of the reasons Mum had been so excited about moving here – "All that space!" she'd cried.

Charlie had nodded but they all knew the real reason Mum and Dad were so pleased. The cottage was free. Well, kind of. Mum had inherited it from this woman Charlie had never heard of before. Great-Aunt Bess, she was called. Mum hadn't known her either. The lawyer said it had taken years and years to find Bess's nearest relatives. She didn't have any children so they'd had to trace all the cousins and everything. It turned out Mum was Bess's great-niece once removed, or something or other.

Either way it couldn't have come at a better time. The mortgage on their old flat had been really high and, with Dad out of work, they'd been in trouble. Charlie wasn't supposed to know this, but she did. All you had to do was vaguely pay attention to know how worried Mum and Dad had been. Now here they were in this mess of a cottage, with its weird buzzy walls and a shower that trickled alternately freezing and boiling water.

Charlie headed further into the woods. It was shady amongst the trees. There was a sudden rustle and a flock of crows flew up into the air, squawking and cawing. What was the name for a flock of crows? It was one of those funny ones, like "a parliament of owls". Charlie remembered all in a rush: a murder. A murder of crows. She shivered and walked on.

Chapter Seven

Not in Kansas Any More

Charlie made her way over roots and fallen logs. Feeling a little foolish, she kept an eye out for trails of pebbles, just in case. Soon she came across a wide path. It looked like one way led towards the village – and the other? Charlie shrugged. It probably went on through the forest and out to the A-road. She looked left and right, trying to work out which direction to go.

There was a loud *Caw!* from above her.

Charlie looked up. A crow was sitting on a low branch. It cocked its head to the side and stared at her. Charlie couldn't help feeling she'd seen it before. "Um. Hello," she said. Then she felt like an idiot. She was talking to a bird!

The bird leaned towards her and peered down.

Charlie's eyes followed his beak. Directly below it was a narrow opening through a set of bushes. It wasn't a proper path, just a muddy trail. The crow gave another caw and flew in-between the bushes and away.

Charlie pushed the thorny branches aside. Yes – someone had been this way. The earth seemed a little trodden. She looked at the neat wide path to the village. Well, she reasoned, if someone was going to build a house of sweets, they wouldn't put it on a main route through a forest. It would definitely be off the beaten track.

She squeezed herself through the thorny spikes and followed the crow down the narrow path, which twisted and turned, leading her further into the trees. All at once it opened out and there, in a little clearing, Charlie found a cottage.

It was clearly not made of sweets. It looked as tumbled-down and messy as Charlie's own cottage. In fact, it looked spookily familiar. It was made of the same coloured stone, it also had a little old tower with a crooked rooftop and, just like on Charlie's cottage, the chimney pot was decorated with carvings, only these ones were of crescent moons instead of stars.

At first Charlie thought the cottage was abandoned. It looked far too derelict to live in! But, as she came closer, she saw signs of habitation. Bunches of dried herbs were hanging over the window sills, crystals tied with string twinkled from behind the old glass and there was a collection of bottles on the doorstep that contained a brownish liquid. Charlie inched forward and touched the doorstep with her foot. All at once she felt the buzzing sensation, but even stronger this time, as if an electric cord was plugged into her veins. She jumped back. Then movement from inside the house caught her eye. Charlie stopped breathing. Her legs went squidgy and her scalp prickled like there were thousands of ants dancing on her head.

The door to the cottage slowly opened and Charlie's eyes widened. There stood a tall woman with long black hair and eyes so dark they were almost purple. Her skin looked smooth but there was something old-fashioned about her – her clothes, perhaps. In her patched-up dress and long black gloves she could have walked straight out of the pages of a history book.

"Yes?" she said in a bored voice. "What do you want?"

"Um. . ." Charlie froze. There was a very long pause. She willed her legs to move, or her voice to work. The buzzing feeling was still there, distracting her. She winced and wriggled her shoulders to try and free herself.

The woman raised her eyebrows. She stared hard at Charlie, her eyes narrowing. Then she gave a little nod. "Well. You'd better come in, I guess," she said. "As you're here."

She turned back into the cottage, leaving Charlie on the doorstep.

Charlie rocked on her heels. Pretty much everything pointed to the fact that going in was Not A Good Idea.

1) The cottage was in the middle of nowhere.
2) The buzzing feeling was horrible.
3) If she got in trouble, no one knew where she was.
4) The woman was weird. She could be a witch.

Yes, said a little voice inside Charlie, *she* could *be a witch. Isn't that what you're looking for?*

I wasn't seriously looking for a witch, Charlie's logical voice answered. *I didn't seriously think witches existed.* But she took a step closer, and closer, until somehow she ended up inside the cottage.

The woman was lifting a kettle off the fire. Charlie flicked a glance around the room. The shelves were covered with old jars of herbs and little bottles of liquid. Twigs and leaves were piled up messily, spilling over on to the floor. There were candles everywhere, casting strange shadows on the stone walls.

"Tea?" said the woman, without turning round.

Charlie meant to politely decline but, just as she was trying to pull the words from somewhere deep down inside, she blurted out something completely different. "Are you a w-witch?" she said, all in a rush. Then she clapped her hand over her mouth.

"Yep," said the witch, casually pouring from the pot. "Milk? Sugar?" She leaned forward. Round her neck was a funny necklace – it was a silver star inside a circle.

"Um. Y-yes, er, please," Charlie nodded. She pinched her own arm, hard. Nope, not a dream. "How, I mean, wh-what, er, really? Are you really a w-w-w..." Charlie trailed off.

The witch slurped her tea. "Ahh, that's nice," she said. "Can't beat a good brew." She put down the cup. "How did you know?" Her voice was casual but her purple eyes stared at Charlie and her long gloved fingers twitched in her lap.

Charlie didn't know how to explain it. The logical part of her brain was trying to list the reasons, but it wasn't working. She just knew there was magic there.

"The buzzing," she said finally. "There's a kind of b-b-buzzing."

"Ah," the witch nodded. "Some people get that." She had a sharp, brisk tone to her voice. "Well. Nice to meet you." She stood up and brushed off her skirt. "Got to get on. Loads to do."

"Wait!" said Charlie. "Can you help me?"

The witch shrugged with her mouth.

"It's my v-voice!" Charlie was falling over her words to explain. "I c-c-can't speak. I think I'm cursed..."

The witch grinned in mockery.

"No, no, I AM," Charlie insisted. "A lady c-came to my house."

The witch started laughing. "Oh, that's the best thing I've heard in a while!" she said. "Cursed! Oh, stop! You're making my sides hurt." She sat down hard. "Look, love," she said, "you're not cursed. You just have a stammer."

Charlie's eyes welled up and she blinked frantically to clear them. "I can't m-make friends."

"Well, maybe so," sniffed the witch, "But that's not because of your voice. Nothing wrong with a stammer. That's just how you talk. Part of who you are."

Charlie shook her head. "It feels like a c-c-curse to me," she mumbled, her voice thick.

The witch gave a wry smile. "Believe me, I'd know if

60

you were cursed." She picked up some long reeds and began to plait them. "You're fine." She wound the strands over and under. "Shame about Suzy Evans, though," she paused a moment. Her eyes flicked up to Charlie then down again. "Eliza got her good and proper."

"Who's Eliza? Wait . . . Suzy Evans?" Charlie repeated, grasping for a hold on reality. "Suzy from s-s-s-school?"

"Know her, do you?"

Charlie nodded, "Yes. Yes. . . I'm Charlie," she said all in a rush. "I go to school with S-Suzy. She's c-cursed?"

"Yeah. At her christening." The witch shrugged. "Hey, it happens."

"Her chr-christening?"

"Yep." The witch's voice sounded deliberately light. "Eliza wasn't invited, you see. She got all offended and whatnot. Said Suzy would lose her singing voice the day she turned seventeen." The witch tied off the end of the plaited reed and stretched out her back. "Could've been worse, I guess."

Charlie remembered something: Suzy up on stage in the hall, croaking loudly. "She was s-s-s-s-inging strangely the other day," she said.

"Ah." The witch nodded slowly. "I heard the curse come in on the wind last Sunday morning. It must have started then. I guess Suzy's nearly seventeen."

She counted on her gloved fingers. "Yep – seventeen next Sunday. Oh well. That's the way the cauldron bubbles."

"No ... no ... wait..." Charlie felt a wave of pity. Poor Suzy! Losing your voice was horrible! Charlie remembered her spluttering on the stage, turning red in the face, with everyone looking at her and giggling. She frowned. "Surely you can do s-s-something, um ... Miss ... witch."

"Agatha," the witch answered. "My name's Agatha." Her voice softened slightly. "Look, removing curses isn't easy, you know. It's serious stuff. Besides, I've given up magic."

"Given up?"

"Yeah." Agatha shrugged casually. "It wasn't really working out for me."

"But you-you-you have to h-h-help Suzy," Charlie insisted. "She's a really nice p-p-p-person! She shouldn't be c-c-cursed!"

Agatha waved her hand. "You could have a go yourself, you know, if you can be bothered." She pushed herself out of her chair and turned to the large pot on the fire. As she passed, the hem of her long dress brushed Charlie's ankle. A jolt shot through Charlie. Something inside her shifted.

"I will," she said firmly, taking herself by surprise. She stood up. "T-t-tell me what to do."

Agatha opened a large red book. The pages were dusty and crumbly at the edges. She flicked through until she came to a drawing. "See this plant?" she said. Charlie came closer. She blinked – the buzzing was so strong around Agatha. It darted to and fro all over Charlie's body. Charlie clenched her teeth. The witch seemed to sense her discomfort. "Don't fight it," she said gently. "Just let it wash over you. Feel its power; feel its warmth."

Charlie's gaze locked on the witch. Slowly the buzz settled down, curling into the pit of her tummy like a lazy cat. Heat spread across her back and her shoulders dropped down, relaxed.

"Right, here we go," said Agatha, pointing to a drawing, "white heather. *Erica carnea* f. *alba*. It blooms in early spring. You need to pick it at moonlight and make a small bouquet. It'll ward off evil. Don't get your hopes up, though. It won't remove the curse, but . . ." she shrugged ". . . it might hold it off a bit."

"OK." Charlie looked at the drawing and tried to fix the image of the little white plant in her mind.

"Disguise yourself as an old peddler woman and give Suzy the flower."

Charlie hesitated. "Um . . . could I just t-t-tie it to her locker?"

Agatha shrugged and waved her hand. "Meh. Whatever."

So that's how Charlie found herself, in the moonlight, on a bit of open land, hunting for a tiny white flower.

What on earth am I doing? she asked herself for the millionth time. The whole thing felt like a weird dream.

Charlie pulled her coat tighter and waved her torch around. There must be heather somewhere here.

Caw! The crow flew overhead.

"Not you again!" said Charlie. She put her hands on her hips. "Well? Do you know where it is?"

The bird swooped down and settled on a bush. Charlie moved closer. On the bush was a patch of white. She crouched and shone her torch.

Tiny white flowers shone back at her. She brushed her hand across the top of the heather and, as it sprang into place, one group of flowers seemed to glow more than the others. Charlie felt a low tingle. She pulled her scissors out of her rucksack and snipped off some sprigs. "Thanks." She grinned at the bird and it flew off into the night sky.

*

At home, Charlie laid the heather on her bed. She was a

bit nervous about the idea of putting it on Suzy's locker. It had to look nice – she didn't want to freak Suzy out! She chose the best sprig, washed it and tied it with some red ribbon from Mum's ribbon box. Then she neatened the flowers and looked at the posy. Yes, it looked pretty now but . . . it was just a normal bunch of flowers. How was it going to work magic?

Charlie frowned and picked up her pen. She'd seen symbols all over Agatha's cottage – they were carved in the woodwork or hanging from the window frames. There was one she remembered in particular: a triangle inside a circle, with a smiling sun inside. She doodled it on the bottom of the red ribbon. Would that help?

"Please work," she whispered. "Please help Suzy." Charlie jumped as she felt another tingle. Were the flowers glowing a bit brighter now? No. Surely that was just a trick of the light.

Chapter Eight
It Was All Lellow

The next morning Charlie woke up early. The events of the previous day were swirling around her head. Did she really meet an actual witch? Did she really stay up half the night making a posy of flowers? Everything was upside down in her mind. Yet somehow it all made sense. For the first time in ages, she felt like she knew what she was doing – what her role was that day. Her job was to tie those flowers to Suzy's locker and save Suzy's singing voice.

She jumped out of bed and packed her things. She was the first one downstairs, so she put the kettle on and made herself a packed lunch.

"Whoah!" said Dad as he walked in, pretending to be shocked at the sight of her.

"Very funny," said Charlie.

"No, seriously, what are you doing upright at this time of day?"

"I'm just g-g-getting ready for school," said Charlie. "Do you want tea? The kettle's boiled."

Dad handed Annie to Charlie. She felt all warm and soft in her bunny pyjamas.

"Morning, Annie," said Charlie. Annie snuggled closer and nuzzled in.

"Ha! She just wiped snot on your neck!" Matt laughed from the doorway.

"Did she? Ew! Annie!"

Dad handed Charlie a bit of kitchen roll and took Annie back. Charlie poked her tongue out at her sister and Annie giggled.

"What are you d-doing today, Dad?" Charlie asked as she buttered her toast.

"The walls, I think," he said "Then tomorrow I can get the worktops up and oil them. It's going to look fantastic in here!"

He picked up *Restoring Your 17th Century Home* and enthusiastically thumbed through the pages.

Once Charlie had crunched her last bit of toast, she wiped her hands on an old rag.

"Careful!" Dad looked up from his book. "That's covered in white spirit."

"Yuk."

"Snot and white spirit? That's what all the girls are wearing," said Matt, flinging on his coat.

Mum whirled into the kitchen. "Come on, come on!" she yelled. "Let's gooooo!" She kissed Dad goodbye. "You've got Annie all day today, remember?"

"Oh, yes," said Dad. "Come on, Munchkin," he said, tickling her. "Let's get you dressed. You can help me paint."

Today, instead of her usual trick of hiding in the library until the first bell went, Charlie hung about in the corridor. Suzy's locker had to be around here somewhere, near the Year Twelve and Thirteen common room. She leaned back against the wall and tried to look casual. There was a low tingle coming from her bag at her feet. She couldn't wait to use the posy!

The bell rang and a crowd came flooding out of the common room. Yes! There was Suzy! She had stopped one, two, three, four lockers along (Charlie made a note in her head). Minutes later the corridor was empty.

As quick as she could, Charlie pulled out the little posy and hooked the red ribbon round the locker handle.

"What are you doing?"

Charlie's heart skipped. She turned to see Kat looking at her with narrowed eyes. A fleeting thought ran through Charlie's head: she really did look very cat-like.

"Um ... n-nothing." Charlie whipped the posy into her coat pocket before Kat could see. "I th-th-thought it was my l-l-locker."

The girl blinked slowly, her green eyes huge under the enormous glasses. "I'll be watching you," she said, her Welsh voice low and musical.

Charlie dashed down the corridor and burst into English.

"Ah, Miss Samuels. Nice of you to join us," said Miss Robbins.

The class giggled and someone murmured "Rumpelstiltskin". There was another bout of laughing. Charlie's face burned bright red as she took her seat.

This is stupid, Charlie told herself. Agatha, the heather, the curse... None of it was true. Her new-found purpose left her like the rush of air from a popped balloon. That woman in the forest was probably having a good laugh about the whole thing now. For goodness' sake, she had followed a *crow*. A CROW! She squeezed her nails into her palm.

For the rest of the day she kept her head down, avoiding Kat and staying well away from Suzy. The best

70

thing, Charlie told herself on her walk home, would be if she could just try for once to be normal.

"Hey! Charlie! Look what I've done!" Dad opened the door to the kitchen with a flourish.

Charlie glanced around the room. The walls were a loud canary yellow.

"Gorgeous, eh?" said Dad, proudly. "Special offer at B&Q! No idea why no one else wanted this colour!"

Charlie didn't answer that last bit. "It's great," she said, summoning enthusiasm.

"Thanks, love," said Dad, "Oh, can you do me a favour while I tidy up here? Can you fetch some bits of kindling from the forest? I haven't got time to chop any more wood and Annie's asleep upstairs so I can't leave her."

"Sure," said Charlie, "I'll just get ch-ch ... dressed."

Once she was out of her uniform, Charlie headed out the back door to the end of the garden. She climbed over the wall and into the woods.

There was the crow again.

"Go away," said Charlie crossly. But it wouldn't. It followed her around, flitting from branch to branch as she looked for twigs on the forest floor. Every time she found one it hopped on to it, blocking her way.

"OK, fine," Charlie said at last. "I'll go and see Agatha. That's what you want, isn't it?"

She pushed through the thorny bushes and walked quickly up to Agatha's door. It was already open.

"Hello?" called Charlie.

"Ah," said Agatha. "You came back."

The second she walked into Agatha's lounge, Charlie felt muddled all over again. It felt so familiar: the smell of herbs and smoky fire. And the buzzing – well, she was getting used to that too. It had become more like a warm feeling in her tummy. She looked around the room. It felt right ... as if she belonged here. Or somewhere like here.

Then the memory of Kat confronting her came flooding back and Charlie screwed up her face.

"So," said Agatha coolly. "Did you pick the heather?"

"Yes," said Charlie. "But I didn't put it on her l-l-locker."

"Hmm?" Agatha was busy mixing some kind of soup. She pulled up her tattered sleeves and stirred the pot round and round on the fire.

"Someone s-s-saw me," Charlie said in a small voice. It sounded like a lame excuse now.

"Be careful." Agatha's voice was sharp. "People don't

like witchcraft. It scares them and that fear. . ." Her face darkened. "That fear makes them do terrible things."

Charlie stared at her.

"Now. Let's see it." Agatha wiped her gloves on her long, jagged dress and held out a hand. Charlie felt in the pocket of her coat. Yes, it was still there. She passed it to Agatha, feeling suddenly shy.

The witch unwrapped the tissue and looked at the posy. She turned it over in her hands and sniffed it. She touched the neat bow of the red ribbon and played with the end. Then she saw the little doodle. "Where did you see this symbol?" she asked.

Charlie blushed. What had possessed her to put that squiggle on the ribbon? "Um. . ." She pointed to a bit of woodwork. The symbol was carved into the bark.

"Hmph."

There was silence for a while. The only sound was the spitting of the fire. Charlie wondered whether she had offended Agatha. Maybe the symbol was something personal? Maybe Agatha would think Charlie had copied her in mockery. Her stomach churned.

Agatha's voice broke into Charlie's thoughts. "It's called a sigil. It's an old symbol used in magic. You chose well; that one is for protection."

Charlie breathed out slowly.

"If you've been spotted with the heather, you can't use it again." She looked into the fire and mumbled as if talking to herself. "No . . . what would be next? What would be a better test. . . ? Ah. . ."

She turned from the fire and scribbled something on a piece of paper.

"You could have a go at this, if you like. Doubt it'll work though. It's a powder." She gave the note to Charlie. "Collect everything on this list and grind it up. Bring it back tomorrow night and I'll tell you how to use it."

Charlie nodded. Somehow, in Agatha's cottage, it was very easy to believe in magic: in spells, curses and witches. She folded the note and put it in her pocket.

"Be careful," Agatha warned. "Don't get seen again."

On the way home Charlie gathered the kindling for Dad.

"Thanks," he said as she delivered her armful of twigs. "Can you watch Annie for me till Mum gets home? I need to clean myself up." He had splashes of canary yellow all over his face. He looked like he'd been swimming in mustard.

"Sure!" said Charlie. "Come on, Annie. Let's put on a m-m-movie."

She settled down on the sofa with her notepad. *The Wizard of Oz* had only just started up when:

"It's raining, Charlie!"

Annie had poured water all over the freshly sanded pile of kitchen worktops. It was dripping off the sides. Charlie sighed and mopped it up. Then she sat back down and opened Agatha's note. She looked at the first ingredient:

1 eggshell

Well, that shouldn't be too hard.

There was a *beep-beep* sound. Charlie sprang to her feet. Annie had managed to re-programme the new oven Dad had just plugged in, and it was now on full blast.

"Annie!" Charlie pressed all the buttons on the front but it wouldn't go off. "Annie! Annie! Come here!"

"No!"

"Annie. Charlie's not c-c-cross. Just come here and show me what you d-d-did."

But Annie wouldn't be budged. She was playing with her baby dolls, putting them in and out of the empty boxes.

"Good baby. Night-night, baby. Baby sleep now. Morning, baby!"

Charlie sighed. She pressed a few more buttons and the oven switched off. *Phew.*

Charlie sat back down on the sofa. Beside each item on the list, she made a note of where to find it:

1 eggshell (kitchen)
1 sprig of lavender (front garden)
2 pinches of orange peel (buy oranges)
3 drops of blue candle wax (village shop?)
1 sprinkle of sandalwood (village shop?)
Sulphur (village shop?)

The front door opened. Mum was home. "Hi!" she called.

"We're in here!" Charlie called back.

Mum pulled off her coat. "Wow!" she cried. "Look at that kitchen! Gorgeous colour!"

Charlie rolled her eyes at Annie.

"Lellow," said Annie seriously.

"Yes," said Charlie, "it's v-v-very lellow."

Chapter Nine

Toil and Trouble

That day in school, all Charlie could think about was the list of ingredients. The hours seemed to drag and it felt like weeks before final bell rang. She fingered the note in her pocket. Last night she'd managed to find the eggshell (from one of Suzy's Golden Goose eggs) and the lavender from the garden. Now all she needed was:

Orange peel
Blue candle
Sandalwood
Sulphur

She could get the orange from the supermarket, and surely Moonquest was the best place for those last three?

Charlie wasn't exactly sure what sulphur was. She just knew it was famous for smelling awful.

Charlie passed the common room. The sound of beautiful singing came drifting out.

*"Where happy little bluebirds fly...
...Beyond the rainbow, why—
crroooooaaaak..."*

Cold shot through Charlie's veins. It was Tuesday. There were five days till Sunday; five days until Suzy turned seventeen.

Charlie leaned against the common room door and breathed out. She closed her eyes and then opened them quickly. Someone was watching her.

She looked around: Kat was standing a little way along the hall, squinting her eyes again like there was something funny going on. Charlie backed into a side door and then ran down the stairwell and out of the building.

She hurried towards the high street and didn't stop until she was right inside the supermarket. *Phew. Safe.* She spent a while looking at the oranges. If it was peel she needed, then it was probably best to pick the smoothest one, wasn't it? Charlie ran her hands over the fruit. One was a little less bumpy than the others. Yes. That felt right. She counted out her money and fed it into the self-service checkout.

Then it was straight to Moonquest. She pushed the door open and stepped inside. The shop smelled of vanilla today. Charlie followed her nose to an incense stick burning on a side counter. Next to it were other flavours: coconut, rose, apple – and sandalwood. She frowned. The list said a "sprinkle" of sandalwood. You couldn't sprinkle an incense stick, could you? She scanned the shelves... Ah! There was sandalwood powder! She took a sachet. On the back it said:

50g Sandalwood powder: for soothing and healing, as an antiseptic and disinfectant. Mix to a paste with milk or rosewater and apply to skin.

The blue candle was easy – there were loads of them sitting on a shelf. That left the sulphur. Charlie couldn't see it anywhere. Her stomach dropped. She'd have to ask at the counter. She looked over; the ponytail guy was leaning over doing a crossword. There was no one else in the shop. It was the perfect time.

Charlie took a step forward. Silently her tongue practised the "s" for sulphur.

Ponytail looked up. "Hey," he said, "what can I do you for?"

"Um. . ." Charlie froze.

S, her brain was screaming. *Just say the S!*

"Uh. . ." She bit her tongue to force it to behave. It was no use. Charlie felt like her jaw was locked. The word was somewhere behind her breastbone, as if stuck there for ever.

She ran out of the shop and on to the green. There she sat, with tears in her eyes, hiding behind a tree in case anyone saw her. Then she looked down. To her horror she was still holding the sandalwood and the candle! Ponytail was going to think she was a shoplifter!

She gasped in panic. Look what her stammer was doing to her! Charlie didn't care what Agatha had said; she felt more cursed than ever.

Get a grip, she told herself. She forced herself to breathe in and out steadily, to focus on the letters the way her old speech therapist, Lucy, had taught her. *Come on, you can do this,* she said in her head. *You have to go back in there.*

She rose to her feet and, before she could chicken out, she walked back into the shop.

"S-s-s-sorry," she said, handing Ponytail the items.

"That's fine." Ponytail spoke to her really slowly, as if

she didn't understand English. "Now, what was it you wanted earlier?"

Charlie took a deep breath. "S-s-s. . ."

"Soap? Star signs? Salve?"

Ponytail was making it worse. Charlie frowned in frustration. She could feel her eyes tearing up again. The bell of the shop door went and Charlie panicked. Someone else had come in! In a rush she snatched the pen out of Ponytail's hand and scribbled down: *Sulphur.*

"Sulphur?" Ponytail raised his eyebrows, "I think I've got some powder down here somewhere." He rummaged around under the desk.

Charlie turned slightly to see if she could see who the new person was. Hopefully it was no one who knew her. Her face flushed hot as she caught a glimpse of bright red hair: it was Kat!

"Aha!" said Ponytail. "Here you go!"

Charlie fumbled in her pocket for her money. She scooped the ingredients into her rucksack and sped out of the shop, leaving the door jangling behind her.

"Hi!" She could hear Kat calling after her but Charlie didn't stop.

Luckily Dad was out. He'd left a note:

Gone to DIY store.

Charlie admired the new kitchen counters. Dad had done a great job! The room was beginning to look like an actual kitchen: a bright-yellow kitchen, but a kitchen all the same.

Charlie chopped up the orange peel and lavender as finely as she could. Now to mix in the rest. Agatha had said to grind the mixture, but Charlie couldn't find anything to use. She really needed one of those pestle and mortar things. *Hang on. . .* Charlie remembered seeing something. *What was it. . . ? Oh yes!* When she'd helped Dad in the garden the other day she'd noticed a funny old marble bowl.

Charlie opened the back door and climbed through the nettles and weeds. Leaning on its side, amongst a pile of old bottles, was a heavy, round bowl. It looked like an over-sized mixing bowl. Charlie puffed as she pulled it upright. She wiped the marble free of snails and mud and felt a little tingle of excitement. The bowl was lovely and smooth – perfect for grinding herbs in! She looked around for some kind of handle or something to crush them with. Ahead of her was the old apple tree, the one with the troll-face in its bark. Charlie poked her tongue out at the troll and looked on the grass for fallen branches. There was one! A nice thick one! She pulled it free of weeds and carried it back to the marble bowl.

She tipped in the chopped orange and lavender, the empty eggshell, the funny-smelling sulphur and the sweet sandalwood. Then she pressed down hard with the branch, crushing and crunching everything again and again until it began to make a powder. As she mixed she concentrated hard. *I hope this works,* she said to herself, remembering Suzy's croak earlier that day.

Charlie's arm was beginning to ache. She stopped to rest for a moment and peered into the bowl. The powder was much finer now, a lovely golden colour from the sandalwood. She felt a bubble of happiness expand inside her and she caught herself grinning.

She looked at Agatha's list again. There was just one last thing left to add:

3 drops of blue candle wax

Charlie lit the candle and tipped it on to its side so the flame caught the wax. It dripped into the bowl: one, two, three drops. There was a hiss and a flash of blue. Charlie jumped as a surge of electricity ran through her bones. She jerked back, her heart hammering inside her chest. A thrill of excitement spread from her toes to her head.

The mixture looked richer somehow. It seemed to glow slightly in the sunshine. Carefully she spooned it into one of the empty bottles propped up against the old cottage. Done! Now she just had to show it to Agatha.

Charlie felt proud of her little bottle of powder. As she squeezed between the bushes on the path to Agatha's house, she found she was desperate to show it off. She knocked at the cottage door and pushed it open. "Agatha?" she called.

"Yep, yep," came an answer from the lounge.

Charlie went in. The crow was sitting on the arm of the chair.

"Is-is-is that yours?" Charlie asked.

"Hopfoot? He doesn't belong to me, but we're friends," Agatha replied. "I knew his mother." Hopfoot bent his head and Agatha stroked her fingers down his neck and back.

"I've made the p-p-powder," Charlie announced.

Agatha held out her hand. Her eyes widened when she saw the bottle. "Where did you get this?"

"It was ou-ou-outside our house," Charlie explained, "in our g-garden."

"I see," said Agatha. She turned the bottle over in her hands. A funny expression crossed her face – a little wince of pain – and then, as quickly as it had appeared, it was gone. When she looked at Charlie again, her purple eyes seemed darker.

She undid the bottle and took a sniff.

"Not bad," she said. She took another sniff. "Apple?" She lifted her eyebrows.

Charlie nodded. "I u-u-used wood from the ap-p-p-ple tree to grind it."

Agatha nodded again.

"Is-is that OK?"

"Apple is good for healing." Agatha put the stopper back on the bottle. "Now. You need to sprinkle it on to Suzy," she said. "Don't get your hopes up. You know what they say," she said as she shrugged, "*not every spell works a charm.*"

Chapter Ten

I'll Get You, My Pretty

On her way to school, Charlie went over her list of possible strategies for sprinkling the powder on to Suzy:

Follow Suzy into the loo and blow powder over her cubicle. (Flaw: hard to know when Suzy will need a wee.)

Pretend to trip over and accidentally pour it on to Suzy. (Downside: I'll look like an enormous klutz.)

Place a cup over a doorway so it falls on Suzy as she walks in. (What if she isn't the first one through the door?)

Put it in her umbrella so when she

opens it the powder will fall on her.
(What if she doesn't have an umbrella?)
   Put it into her hat (see flaw with
umbrella).
   Blow it on to her from a distance
using a specially constructed long
funnel.

She wasn't particularly happy with any of the plans. One thing was clear though: she would need to find Suzy when no one else was around. Unfortunately this was not easy. Suzy always had people hanging about her, chatting and giggling.

She'd kept an eye out for Suzy at first break, but there had been no sign of her. It was going to be hard enough to find a way to get the powder on to Suzy as it was, let alone if she couldn't actually *find* her.

The bell rang for lunch and Charlie *still* hadn't seen Suzy. Maybe she was ill? Maybe she was on a school trip? Charlie chewed her lip. There was only one thing for it: she'd have to go into the canteen to look for her.

Ever since her first day – the day her voice had stopped – Charlie had avoided the canteen. There were too many people sitting together in groups, people who actually had friends to hang out with. Charlie would look like such a loser sitting on her own. Or worse, someone might sit with her and try to talk to her! She cringed as she pictured it. No – the library was much safer. It was nice and quiet and, although she wasn't supposed to eat in there, if she hid her sandwich halfway down her jumper she could take sneaky bites when the librarian wasn't looking.

But today – today she had to face the canteen. She pulled the heavy door open and slipped in. She remembered what Spiky had said that first day about how Year Twelve and Thirteen always sat at the tables by the window, and she chose a seat near the side, with full view of the Year Twelve table.

From behind her wall of hair Charlie glanced around the room, trying not to make eye contact with anyone. Oh no! There was Kat! She was by herself about three tables away. Her short red hair was decorated with a bright blue scarf, tied in a massive bow that flopped over her forehead. She was playing with her food, making her mashed potato into a large white mountain. Charlie looked away quickly. She spotted Suzy up at the till, swiping her thumb on the reader. Phew! She was here. Now it was just a matter of getting her by herself. Charlie really didn't fancy pouring strange powder on her in front of the whole school.

She watched as Suzy made her way to the Year Twelve table. Suzy looked tired and unhappy. She was pale and there were dark shadows under her eyes. One of her friends got up from the table to hug her. Charlie winced. It was the school show next week – Charlie had seen the posters up everywhere. Today was Wednesday. On Sunday, Suzy would lose her voice, and on Monday night she would be up on stage singing "Somewhere Over the Rainbow". Or, by then, croaking it. Charlie screwed up her fists. She had to find a way to use the powder.

She stood and began to cross the canteen. She would wait for Suzy by the common room. She was bound to go there after lunch, and maybe, Charlie crossed her fingers, maybe she'd be alone. As she passed the tables she saw Kat looking at Suzy with a puzzled expression – no, it was more than puzzled; she looked worried, almost scared, like she thought Suzy was going to suddenly explode or something.

With her head down, Charlie walked past Suzy, out of the canteen and along the corridor. She unzipped her bag as she walked and fished out the bottle of powder. She closed her fingers around the glass, and waited.

A crowd approached, filled with people moving off to sports clubs or music rooms or the playground. Charlie craned her neck to see. Where was Suzy? There! She was there – in the middle of a group, walking towards Charlie. One by one her friends broke off. Soon there was just Suzy and Spiky. This was the moment! With shaking fingers Charlie undid the cork of the bottle. She tipped the powder on to her palm and cupped her hand ready. Forget all the strategies. She was just going to have to throw it and hope she didn't look like a mad person.

Suzy came closer. Time slowed. Charlie could count every footstep. She lifted her fist and drew back her arm to prepare for the throw. She brought it forward and. . .

Oooof!

Next thing she knew, Charlie was on the floor. Someone had pounced on her, knocking her down. She scrambled up but Suzy had gone. The powder was sprinkled all over the floor and, already, people were stepping in it and covering it with dirt and mud from the bottom of their shoes.

"What are you doing to Suzy?" It was Kat, owner of the suspicious face and, it turned out, quite good pouncing skills.

"N-n-n-nothing," Charlie managed.

"Yes you are! I've seen you. You're making Suzy ill."

"N-no-no." Charlie was panicking now.

"Yes you are!"

"I'm h-h-h-helping," Charlie said.

"How?" Kat's freckles merged as she screwed up her face.

"I can't t-t-tell you," Charlie's voice wavered, "But I AM."

Kat put her hands on her hips and narrowed her green eyes. Her blue bow bobbed up and down. "I'm still watching you," she said eventually, and stalked away.

Charlie dashed into the loo. She slammed the cubicle door and locked it tight. Then she sat on the toilet seat and hid her head in her hands. She was running out of time. Five days left. Five days!

Chapter Eleven

Gifts For a Princess

"Sh-she's everywhere I g-g-go!"

Charlie was trying to explain to Agatha how annoying Kat was. It was like she was prowling the corridors, hunting Charlie down, watching her every move. It was weird the way she looked at Suzy too. Her eyes would dart from Suzy to Charlie and her forehead would crinkle up like she was looking at something strange.

Agatha didn't seem to be listening though. She carried on tying bunches of herbs to the window frames. She had her back to Charlie and the laces at the back of her old dress were untangling as she reached up to add the last posy.

There was something else too – something Charlie

hadn't told Agatha. When Kat had pushed her over, Charlie had felt the buzzing feeling again, spreading from her shoulders down to her feet. A moment later it had stopped. She decided she wouldn't say anything to Agatha. Not until she felt it again.

Instead she said, "Wh-what should I do now? I l-lost the powder. And I'm r-r-running out of time."

"Well, I'm not sure you can do much more." Agatha shrugged as she answered. "It's not long till Sunday. Shame though." Her voice softened. "She was a cute baby, Suzy."

"D-d-did you see her?"

"Yep. The whole village was invited to the christening. Well, everyone except Eliza."

"Why wasn't Eliza invited?"

Agatha had a floaty, faraway look in her eyes. "By then Eliza had become very strange," she explained. "She'd hidden herself away from everyone, even me. And *I* was her best friend. That book!" She spat the word crossly and Charlie's eyes widened. "I told her no good would come of it. I told her not to touch dark magic. Tcha!" She took a long breath. "She couldn't help it, I guess. The pull of the dark is so strong, you see. In the end she just gave in to it. Anyway. . ." She shook herself and stood up. "Everyone avoided her.

They thought she was odd. So the Evans family didn't invite her."

"Wh-what happened at the chr-christening?"

"Everyone was giving gifts: you know, photo albums, jewellery, a music box. I gave her a singing voice. . ."

"You did?"

"Yep. Had to whisper the spell, of course. Remember what I told you about not being noticed?"

Charlie nodded.

"I sprinkled the potion on her really quickly, when no one was watching," Agatha said proudly. "One of my finest potions! That girl has been singing like a nightingale for almost seventeen years."

Charlie waited to hear what was coming.

"Then Eliza came in. She was furious she'd been left out. . . I remember. . . The room was busy, everyone was chattering away, and they all went quiet when she swept in. Of course Mrs Evans was really apologetic about the whole thing. She cut Eliza a bit of cake but Eliza was still fuming. She came and sat next to me. 'So,' she said, 'I see they invited you.' Her face was thin and shrivelled and her mouth was pulled tight.

"'Oh, Eliza, don't make a scene,' I told her. 'It's not that important.'

"'They'll pay,' she whispered.

"'Don't be ridiculous. You know the rules: "Magic mustn't harm".'

"Eliza laughed bitterly. 'I can't believe you are quoting that to me! How many fellow witches have been hurt over the years? How many of our ancestors suffered for their powers?'

"'Shush, Eliza,' I said. 'That was long ago. People don't hurt witches anymore. Things are different now.'

"Eliza shook with anger. 'Different? Huh! We witches still hide our gifts. We're still not welcome. Still not open. And you, you just let it happen. You pretend to fit in, Agatha. *I* wouldn't stoop so low.'

"'I'm not pretending; I'm just being friendly.'

"'Liar!' she spat. 'How many people here know you're a witch?'

"I tried to shush her, but she kept on.

"'None of them! Because you are a coward! You smile at them, go to their parties, and all the time you know what people have done to witches in the past, what they might do again. I bet you gave the baby a nice sweet gift for her birth! What did you give her? Beauty? Wit? Grace?'

"'Singing,' I said.

"'Ah, the classic,' she said bitterly.

"'Eliza. Please. Come and see me. Let's talk. It's been

ages.' I put my hand over hers. But she snatched it away."

Agatha turned to Charlie. "I was still reaching out to her, you see. Foolishly I thought it wasn't too late. I thought she would come back to white magic; come back to me."

Charlie stared open-mouthed. Dark magic? White magic? She felt an odd dip in her tummy and her heart was thumping in excitement.

"Then Eliza stood up. She leaned over the cradle and pulled a small bottle from her handbag. I tried to stop her, but she was so fast! And so angry. She was angry with the world, angry with the Evans family and angry with me. The dark magic had hold of her by then and nothing was going to stand in her way. She whispered her curse to the baby."

Agatha clenched her fists. Her voice was tight. "She did it to hurt me, I know." She closed her eyes and quickly opened them again. "Eliza deliberately chose a curse that would undo the gift I'd given. And she bound it tight with the old words:

'Let it be done, as I foretell,
No witch alive can break my spell!'

"Then she swept out of the room. No one saw what had happened, of course, but I knew."

There was a long silence.

"Wh-wh-what happened to Eliza?" Charlie asked.

"She's dead," Agatha answered. "The havoc got her."

Charlie looked puzzled.

"Havoc," Agatha said again. "It's a side product of dark magic. The more dark magic you use, the more unlucky you are."

"H-h-how did she die?" Charlie was almost too scared to ask.

"She choked on an apple."

"Really?"

"Yep. Only a week or so after the christening. Witches might be magic, but we can be stupid too. Anyway," Agatha said, making her voice lighter, "that's what comes of dark magic. Bad luck – bad luck and havoc."

Charlie rubbed her eyes. She clung to one thought. "No-no w-w-witch can take off the spell?" Was that why Agatha needed Charlie, a non-witch, to do it?

"Dark curses are tricksy, and Eliza bound this one tight. I knew I couldn't take it off but after Eliza's death I tried anyway. . ." Agatha slowly drew off her left glove. Charlie gasped. Her little finger! The top bit of Agatha's little finger was missing.

"H-h-how? Wh-what hap-p— happened?" Charlie was falling over her words to get them out fast enough.

"The curse fought back," Agatha said simply. "You can feel it, you know, when you try and draw it out. It's like a force pulling, like you're playing tug of war. Anyway," she shrugged, "the curse won. The binding knew I was a witch."

Charlie's breath caught in her throat.

"And that was the day I gave up magic."

"I didn't know it was so-so-so dangerous."

Agatha's eyes flashed. "Never," she snapped, "never underestimate magic!" She breathed in and out to calm herself. "That's why I'm being careful with you," she said eventually. "Like I told you, the spells you are trying, they can help a bit. They can slow down the curse. But they're not strong enough to take the curse off completely."

Something in Charlie took over. "G-g-give me something stronger," she said. "Please. M-m-maybe I can take the curse off."

Agatha breathed in through her nose deeply. "I have wondered," she said. "The binding said 'no witch alive. . .'" She looked away and seemed to drift off.

Charlie nodded in encouragement. Surely, if she wasn't a witch, then the binding didn't apply to her?

"Well," Agatha said slowly, "there is something stronger you could try. Do you know what a poppet doll is?"

Charlie shook her head.

"It's a small figure used for healing. You make a doll of the person you want to help; it focuses the healing spell you cast." Agatha leaned in. "This is difficult magic, Charlie. It probably won't work."

Charlie rolled her eyes.

Agatha wagged her finger back at her. *"If wishes were broomsticks, devils would fly.* We can't always get what we want. Believe me. I should know." Agatha cleared her throat. "Right. You need to make a doll of Suzy. It can be out of cloth or clay or anything just as long as you think of Suzy when you make it. Wrap it in something Suzy has recently touched. Then you need to make a chalk circle and sit right in the middle of it. Do you still have that blue candle?"

"Yes."

"Light it. Hold the doll and say these words:

Light, light, work your charm,
Keep our Suzy safe from harm.

"You have to really focus on the words. Say them slowly and concentrate, otherwise this won't work."

*

Charlie made the doll from some old curtains Mum was throwing out. They had a faded cherry pattern on them that looked just right for Suzy. She sewed yellow wool for hair. Due to her rubbish sewing skills, the doll barely looked like a girl, let alone like Suzy. Still. Agatha had said that wouldn't matter, as long as Charlie thought about Suzy while she was making it.

It was getting late, and the moon shone through Charlie's window and on to the doll. As she sewed, she had one last practice of the lines:

'Light, light, work your charm,
Keep our Suzy safe from harm.'

In her room, by herself, her voice rang out clear and true.

Carefully Charlie put the doll and the candle into her school bag. Now all she had to do was to get something Suzy had touched to wrap up the doll.

As she put her head on the pillow, the words were still floating around her head. She could see the moon shining down and, closing her eyes, her last thought was that it was glowing strangely bright.

Chapter Twelve

Weird Sisters

Early the next morning Charlie was woken by loud voices.

Mum was having a row with Matt in the room next door. Their voices were muffled but the occasional phrase rose up.

Matt's stroppy: "Aw, Mum, I *already told you* I'll do it tonight."

And Mum's softer: "Daddy and I are just worried. . ."

Charlie pulled her pillow over her head. It must be about the science project *again*. Matt was late handing it in and Mum had been nagging him about it since Monday.

Actually, it was kind of a relief to have Mum and Dad focusing on Matt. It made it much easier for Charlie to get away with sneaking off into the woods, or staying up late to make poppet dolls. Already she was beginning to run out of excuses. She'd used the "I'm just off for firewood" one a few too many times, along with "Oh, I fancy a little walk". Mum's radar would be on to her by now if it weren't for Matt giving her something else to worry about.

They were still listening out for her stutter, though. Charlie had heard Mum and Dad talking about it after dinner last night, when they thought she couldn't hear. Mum was "keeping an eye on it", she said. It was true, Charlie admitted to herself as she got dressed: her stutter was bad. And she still didn't have any proper friends at school. But, what Mum didn't know was that Charlie was dealing with something way more important! Today was Thursday. There were only two school days left till the weekend. Two days to help Suzy. And, for now, that had to take priority.

There was a loud *Caw!* from outside. Charlie opened her window. Hopfoot was sitting on the highest branch of the apple tree. Charlie waved to him and for a moment it looked like he bowed his head in return. Charlie grinned.

The truth was, it wasn't *all* about Suzy. Charlie did want Suzy to be able to sing again, but it was more than that. For the first time in her life, Charlie felt like she was doing something useful.

As she tied her shoelaces she wondered what would happen if Agatha's spell worked. Would it all be over? Would she stop going to see Agatha? Stop helping her with her magic? Surely she couldn't go back to the way she was before. Back to when she didn't know about magic, didn't know about the old cottage in the woods. Charlie couldn't bear the thought of that! She was desperate to learn more about Agatha's world. Maybe she could keep helping Agatha. Didn't witches have assistants sometimes? A non-magical person who helped them? Maybe Charlie could volunteer for that role. If she managed to help Suzy, maybe Agatha would let her run errands for her, or . . . or . . . clean out her cauldron. *Anything.* Charlie didn't care what she did so long as she could still hear about witches and white magic and dark magic and spells and charms and Eliza and Agatha and. . . Oh, there was so much to know! She *had* to persuade Agatha to let her help!

In maths, while everyone was concentrating on nth term numbers, Charlie went over the plan in her head. She had the wonky-looking poppet doll in her bag. Now she needed something of Suzy's to wrap it in. Agatha had said the spell had to be done with something Suzy had recently touched. The stronger the link between Suzy and the object, the better the spell would work. On a spare bit of paper, Charlie made a list of examples Agatha had mentioned:

The object could be a treasured possession of Suzy's. (Might be hard to get this. And to make sure I give it back again.)

Something Suzy has dropped fluid on. (Fluid? Does that mean blood? Snot? Tears? I can't hurt her. Maybe if she has a nosebleed?)

The spell has to be done as soon as possible after Suzy has touched the item. (Note: find somewhere to light the candle. Spare music room? Additional note: get chalk.)

"Ah, Charlotte, you look like you know the answer." Mr Wyatt had his eyebrows raised.

Oh no! What was the question? *Um. . .* She panicked.

"Don't be shy." Mr Wyatt looked at her kindly. "Why don't you just show me what you've been writing down?"

Frantically Charlie covered her list with her arms. There was no way she could let anyone see it. Her heart was beating fast. She had to say something. There were numbers on the whiteboard:

$$5, 8, 14, 23$$

Quickly she worked out the sequence. It was adding the three times table. Three then six then nine, so that meant the answer had to be:

"Thirty-five," she said, surprising herself with how clear her voice sounded.

"Yes." Mr Wyatt smiled and nodded.

Charlie grinned back. She folded up her list and hid it in her bag.

At first break, Charlie looked for Suzy. She wasn't in the common room, she wasn't by her locker and she wasn't in the corridor. She carried on looking for as long as possible, ducking into a doorway now and then to avoid Kat. (*Seriously*, Charlie thought in annoyance, *that girl has the hunting skills of a lioness.*) There were only five minutes to go before the next class and Charlie desperately needed the loo. She gave up looking and dashed into the nearest girls' toilet.

In the cubicle next door, someone was singing softly. There was a loud *crooooaaak* and then a sob. Charlie drew in a breath – it was Suzy! She winced as Suzy cried and cried. She felt awful for her. *The Wizard of Oz* show was on Monday. Suzy couldn't possibly sing up on stage in front of everyone.

When the bell went, Suzy opened her cubicle door. Charlie could hear her pulling a paper towel from the machine. She peered through a tiny crack in the door and watched as Suzy dried her tears and put the towel in the bin. Suzy took a deep breath, like she was gathering up courage, opened the door and left the bathroom.

Charlie dashed to the bin and pulled out the damp paper towel. It still had drips from her tears. It felt a bit like she was stealing something personal from Suzy, but, Charlie reasoned, that was kind of the point. She pushed the towel down into her bag. She needed to do the spell the first chance she had. She opened her timetable. Art was next.

Charlie rushed down the corridor and into the art room.

"So I want you to walk around the school and choose something to draw," Ms Bradley was saying. "It could be a bit of pavement. It could be a view. It could be a section of the canteen or the gym. Think creatively! I want something different – something from an unusual viewpoint. Try not to disturb other lessons. We'll all meet back here in one hour."

There was a mad rush as everyone gathered up their things to head out. Charlie's heart leaped. *Yes!* She was free for an hour. Maybe, if she found a quiet room, she could quickly do the spell and then do her drawing. Ms Bradley would never know!

Charlie went straight to the music corridor. There was a row of practice rooms. She listened at each door until she found an empty one. There! She snuck in and closed the door behind her.

With trembling hands, she pulled her things out of her bag. She drew a wobbly chalk circle on the floor and stepped inside it. She felt a little silly, but there was no one there to see, so she took her place, sitting right in the middle as Agatha had told her.

Carefully, she wrapped the poppet doll in Suzy's paper towel. She made it look neat, as if mini-Suzy was wearing a nice towel-blanket. Then she took out a box of matches and lit the blue candle.

Charlie closed her eyes, breathing slowly, and focused on Suzy. She pictured Suzy's face, imagining her voice singing out clear. A calmness swept over her. She felt a strange pressure building up in her chest. It wasn't a horrible, pressing force; it felt warm and soft and dreamy.

"Light, light, work your charm," she began to say, concentrating on every syllable, every letter.

There was a *whoosh* of air from the music-room door.

Charlie's eyes snapped open and she registered Kat standing in the doorway, staring at her.

From then on things seemed to happen very sluggishly, like a film in slow motion. Charlie reached to shield the poppet doll from view. Her arm hit the candle and it toppled over, setting fire to the paper towel. The doll shot into flames. Those old curtains must have been dry as a bone. She watched in horror as smoke hit the ceiling and:

Drrrinnnnng! Drrrinnnnnng!

It was the fire alarm. Charlie stood up in shock. Suddenly the sprinklers came on.

She looked up and met Kat's bright eyes. To her surprise, the girl moved swiftly into the room. She stamped on the doll to put out the remaining flames. Outside people were thundering past in a panic to get out of the building. Kat turned to Charlie. In the rain of the sprinkler she said, "I don't know what you are up to but you need to stop, now."

Charlie's mouth opened and closed like a fish. Kat went on, "I've seen the glow around Suzy. There's

110

something wrong with her and it's all your fault."

"No," Charlie said at last. "No. . . I mean . . . yes th-th-there is something wrong with S. . . with S . . . S. . ."

Kat waited patiently for Charlie to say the name. She didn't interrupt, or try to fill in the letters. She just waited until finally Charlie could say, ". . . with Suzy. I d-d-don't know about any glow but she's losing her v-voice."

"I noticed," said Kat. Her voice sounded less cross now. She raised her eyebrows in interest.

"I'm trying to h-help her," Charlie said. She let out a long breath.

There was a silence. Kat tilted her head to the side and stared into Charlie's eyes. Then she stepped forward.

"I don't know why, but I believe you," she said, and she touched Charlie's hand.

A bolt of electricity shot along Charlie's veins. For a split second she saw herself through Kat's eyes, as if she was inside Kat's head. She saw a curly-haired girl, with a gap between her front teeth, standing soaking wet in a scruffy school uniform. It wasn't like looking in the mirror – it was more than that. For a brief moment, Charlie saw herself as *Kat* saw her. Kat's Charlie looked scared and anxious. Her brow was furrowed in thought. Her face was smoky from the candle.

The feeling passed a moment later.

111

Charlie stepped back in shock. Kat's face was pale. "Did you just see. . . ? I mean, I saw inside your head . . . or. . . What happened?" Kat's voice trembled.

Charlie's mouth silently opened and shut. She had no answer.

"I'll help you," said Kat suddenly. "With Suzy, I mean."

"What are you two girls doing?" Miss Robbins was in the doorway. She sounded furious. "Get out of here now! You should be lining up in the playground with the others." Her eyes swept around the room. Kat quickly stepped in front of the candle to hide it.

"Out! Now!" Miss Robbins shouted and headed on to check the next room.

Charlie hurriedly pushed the candle into her bag and grabbed the sodden, half-burned doll. Then she followed Kat out of the door and into the playground.

Chapter Thirteen

No Witch Alive

"And I expect the culprit to come to my office by the end of the day."

The head's voice was icy with anger.

Charlie looked at her feet. She'd have to own up. As soon as everyone had gone back to class, she'd knock at the head's door and tell him the fire alarm was her fault. She felt sick at the thought of it. And she'd need a good story about that candle: why she had it, why she'd lit it, that sort of thing. She chewed her lip and ran through options:

It was my birthday. (No. The school
Know my date of birth.)
   It was someone else's birthday.
(Well, yes, but whose?)

It was dark and I had to light a
candle to see. (Nah. That's stupid.)
    I was doing a science experiment.
(No, that won't work. I was supposed
to be in art, not science.)

Come on, think! Charlie screwed up her face. She
needed something good. She couldn't just blurt out,
"Well, yes I lit a candle, but it was just so I could chant
a spell and save Suzy from a curse put on her by a
witch!"

At once, Ms Bradley's words floated back to her:
"Draw something from an unusual viewpoint."

Maybe that could be why she lit the candle? She
could say she wanted to draw something by candlelight!
Charlie felt a bit guilty using Ms Bradley's project for her
own purposes but, as she knocked at the head's door,
she knew she really had no choice.

Five minutes later Charlie was being told off by
the head – "so unlike you", "really let yourself down",
"not what I expect from students at this school", "very
disappointed", "your parents will be notified", and, worst
of all:

"Charlotte, I cannot have anyone playing with fire in
the school. The rules are quite clear on this. I'm going to

have to formally exclude you for one day. Now, I'd like you to use your time tomorrow to think about what you have done. I'll see you on Monday."

Tomorrow was Friday! Charlie's last day to see Suzy! Her heart sank. She had failed. She wiped a tear from her eye and the head's voice softened slightly. "Why don't you have a chat with Mrs Davis before you go? She's the school counsellor. I think it might do you some good."

Charlie nodded miserably.

"What's wrong?" asked the counsellor in a gentle voice. "Is there anything you want to tell me about?"

Charlie fought the urge to scream:

1) I have a stammer.
2) I have no friends.
3) Witches exist.
4) There's a curse on Suzy Evans.
5) I saw into another person's head!!!!!!!!

"Er... No, n-n-nothing," she said.

The counsellor's face changed. Charlie had seen that "concerned" look before. All grown-ups did it when they heard her stammer. Children tended to smirk or giggle.

That was embarrassing, sometimes painful, but it was not as bad as what adults did. With their faces full of pity and their deliberately slowed-down voices, they were somehow worse.

The counsellor nodded kindly and wrote something in her notebook. Great. Now it was on record that Charlie had a stammer. Charlie swallowed hard.

"You know, Charlotte," the counsellor said, leaning forward with her hands on her knees, "my door is always open if you want to talk."

Charlie nodded and gave a weak smile.

"Good. Mr Clarke says you can go home now, dear. We really want you to think about what happened today. It was foolish and dangerous, and I have a feeling you're not telling us the full story."

Charlie bit her lip. There was a long silence.

"OK, then," the counsellor sighed in disappointment. "Off you go, Charlotte. We'll speak soon."

Phew. Charlie got out of there as fast as she could. She walked down the corridor and straight through the front door, keeping her head bowed and her hair over her face.

She stamped crossly along the high street, poked her tongue out at Moonquest, and marched straight towards the woods. All the excitement she'd had about magic that morning had gone. Agatha, Suzy, spells: nothing but trouble! She'd been at school nearly two weeks and she'd been excluded. *Excluded!* She'd never been in so much trouble in her whole life! How was she going to explain it to Mum and Dad?

And Agatha? She was supposed to be helping Charlie. *She's my witch*, Charlie muttered to herself, *I found her. She should help* me. *Me and my stammer and my life.* But no; Agatha had Charlie running around looking like a loony and getting in a whole heap of trouble. Charlie fumed as she stomped.

Hopfoot was circling above her as she shoved her way through the bushes. Charlie glared at him. "Magic!" she spat out. "Pah!" Her anger was boiling up inside her. She banged hard with her fist on the old cottage door and it flew open.

Agatha was hanging crystals.

"I'm not d-d-doing any of it any . . . any . . . any more," Charlie announced. She folded her arms and flung herself into a chair.

Agatha didn't say a word. She just carried on tying string around the strange-shaped gems.

"I mean what's the p-p-p-point?" Charlie went on. "No one knows what I'm re-re-re-really doing. Everyone just thinks-thinks-thinks-thinks I'm up to no good." She shouted at Agatha, "I l-l-look like an idiot w-w-w-ith p-p-osies and p-p-powder and d-d-dolls!" Her throat felt like it was closing up. She shut her mouth and glared at Agatha.

Agatha reached up and tied the string around the window latch. "It's a difficult path, the one you have chosen."

"Huh?" Charlie stamped her foot. "I d-d-didn't ch-ch-choose anything!" she burst out. "You are supposed to help m-m-m-m-me!" She shouted the last word.

Agatha sighed, "There's nothing wrong with you."

This was so unfair that Charlie just screamed: "Grrraaaaahhh!"

Agatha didn't even raise her eyebrows.

Tears prickled Charlie's eyes. She put her head in her hands and gave a sob. Still, Agatha said nothing. She just waited and waited until Charlie was calmer. When Charlie finally lifted her head, Agatha handed her a handkerchief and said, "A stammer isn't a curse." Charlie sniffed. "Don't lose sight of the real problem here. It's Suzy who needs help, not you."

Heat filled Charlie's face. She thought of Suzy crying in the toilets that morning. Of course she had to help her! Even if it did mean looking like an idiot, or getting in trouble. Only: "I h-h-haven't m-m-managed a single sp-spell," she said in a small voice.

"Magic isn't easy, Charlie. It's not going to happen at the drop of a wand."

Charlie could hear it in Agatha's voice: she was about to give up. Charlie suddenly felt her world slipping away.

"I-I-I'll try again!" she said in a desperate rush.

Agatha breathed in for a moment, considering something. Then she shook her head.

"What?" said Charlie.

"It's too dangerous."

"Please?"

"No," said Agatha firmly. "You're not ready. It would take a powerful witch."

"Y-y-you could help me," said Charlie. "W-we could do it together."

"No," Agatha snapped. "The binding would know and you'd get hurt." She blew out hard. "I haven't done magic for seventeen years," she said grumpily. "I never want to use it again."

"W-why? I d-don't understand."

Agatha sighed. "I stopped after Eliza died," she said eventually. "She was my friend. I tried everything and even my best magic couldn't help her. I couldn't bring her back to white magic. I couldn't stop the havoc coming. And I couldn't break the curse. I won't use magic again."

A thought hit Charlie. "It-it said, 'no witch alive'." Her heart beat faster. Suddenly she knew what to do! "We-we-we could f-find a witch who wasn't alive sssssseventeen years ago!"

Agatha looked at Charlie. "I have thought of that," she said. "Over the last seventeen years I've hoped to find someone. But witches are very rare. Not many have the gift. And those that do don't always want to work on developing it."

"G-g-gift?"

"True witches are born with talent – with a special ability."

Wow! Charlie felt a wash of envy.

"But it's unusual. Magic can skip many generations before it's seen again. The problem is, a lot of witches died. There aren't many left with the talent to pass on."

"H-how did they d-die?"

Agatha sighed. "There used to be a whole community of witches," she said, "hundreds of years ago. They lived out on Broom Hill, in the west of town. In those days there weren't proper doctors, you know. People came to witches for help with everything: for love spells or healing or even just to make their crops grow better. They were part of village life . . . until *Hopkins*." She spat the last word.

"Who?"

"Matthew Hopkins." Agatha's face grew dark. "The witch hunter. It was his job to find witches, you see. Find them and destroy them. He did horrible things, even to good witches. One day, many years ago, he came to this village."

"What h-h-h-happened?" Charlie was perched on the edge of her seat.

"The witches hid. Some headed for the caves, some to other towns. Some were caught. Others came here, to the woods." She looked around. "This used to be a witch's cottage back in the seventeenth century. It's been handed down from witch to witch through generations." Agatha's voice dropped low. "Sometimes, when I look at the fire, I picture what it must have been like to be a witch in those days, hiding here, in fear for your life."

Charlie swallowed.

"Eliza's cottage was ancient, too. It used to be the *Akelarre* – the meeting place for the coven. After Hopkins, the remaining witches gathered there in secret to celebrate the sun and moon days."

Charlie nodded, transfixed.

"In time, many of the witches died. They had no children to pass their gift on to. Years later, Eliza and I carried on the coven traditions in her cottage, in the

Akelarre, on our own. But then one day, a long time ago, Eliza found an old journal bricked up inside a secret hole. It described the witch trials and the escape of the few sisters who made it out. It . . . it was. . ." Agatha searched for the word. "Graphic." She cleared her throat. "It really affected Eliza. She read the diary over and over, and it made her angrier and angrier. Along with the journal was an ancient book: a grimoire."

Charlie looked confused.

"Grimoire," Agatha said again. "It's a witch's book of spells. This is my one." She waved her hand at the big red book behind her. "Eliza wouldn't show me the grimoire she found. But it must've been written by someone who practised dark magic." Agatha's face twisted. "Eliza became obsessed with it. It drew her in. Dark magic can do that. It's very powerful and it feeds on anger and hate. Over the following years Eliza changed. She withdrew from everyone. She grew paranoid. She was sure people were going to track her down and hurt her. She changed her name over and over again, just in case. Near the end she wouldn't even see me."

Agatha stared into the fire. Her thoughts were far away. "I tried to help her. But she was so angry: angry about how witches had been treated, angry about the modern world. She wouldn't answer the door to me; she wouldn't talk to me. She wouldn't use the cottage as a meeting place any more and she hid herself away in the cellar, making dark potions and spells, each one more dangerous than the last. And then, when I saw her at the christening, I knew something was really wrong. The havoc was already starting to show."

"Wh-what do you mean?"

"She was thin and old. She looked shrivelled, like the hate was taking hold of her. Poor Eliza. Once she'd gone that far it was hard to come back. The curse she put on Suzy was the last spell she ever cast." Agatha sighed.

"So are th-there any new w-witches? One that was b-b-born after the curse?"

"The trouble is, being a witch is about more than just having the gift. You have to practise. It takes patience and care and time. Even if I found someone with the gift now, there wouldn't be time to train her up. I'd be putting her in danger. No. The most we can do is try to hold the curse off for as long as possible." Agatha looked glum. "Tcha!" She waved her hand. "Maybe it's for the best. Being a witch is dangerous. People don't like us. Like I told you: make sure you're never seen with magic."

Charlie thought of Kat seeing her with the candle, and she squirmed. "Um. . ." She hesitated.

"Someone has spotted you with a spell, haven't they?"

Charlie winced in answer. Then she nodded. "It's that g-girl – Kat. She saw me with the p-p-powder. And with the c-c-candle."

Agatha pursed her lips.

"It gets worse," Charlie admitted. "She ssssays she knows there's something wrong with Suzy. She sssssays Suzy has a funny g-g-glow."

"Does she, now?" Agatha stared closely at Charlie.

"And..." Charlie blurted before she could help herself, "when she touched my hand sssomething funny happened." The words were tumbling out of her now, falling over themselves to get out. "I could ssssee inside her head!" Charlie cried.

Agatha stood up sharply. "I need to meet her," she said. Her voice was urgent. "When can you get her here?"

Charlie breathed fast. She'd never heard Agatha sound so desperate. Kat. Kat must have the gift. *She's a witch!* That's why she could make Charlie see inside her head! Charlie felt a stab in her heart. Lucky, lucky Kat!

"When?" Agatha asked again.

Charlie winced. If only she hadn't been suspended! Now she was banned from going to school tomorrow! She didn't have Kat's phone number. Where did she live? How could she find her?

"Matt!" Charlie cried in a flash of inspiration. Her

brother knew everyone. He could find her at school tomorrow and send her a message from Charlie.

"I think I can b-bring her tomorrow," said Charlie.

"Good." Agatha nodded. "Then we might have a chance at stopping this curse."

Charlie frowned. *Hadn't Agatha just said there was no time to train a new witch?* It didn't make sense . . . or maybe . . . maybe Kat was some kind of super-powerful witch? Charlie swallowed down another stab of envy.

Chapter Fourteen

A Familiar Feeling

Mum and Dad were furious.

They shouted for ages about the candle and the fire alarm and the exclusion.

Charlie apologized so many times she felt like a performing parrot.

Then Mum hugged her and Dad hugged her and Annie hugged her, and everything felt a bit better.

After dinner she knocked on Matt's door. "Can you do me a f-favour?"

Matt raised his eyebrows, immediately suspicious.

"P-p-please? I'll help you w-w-with science." That project was now well overdue and Matt *still* had loads to do on it.

He grinned. "Yes! Thank you!" He rummaged around

and handed her a piece of paper with drawings of faces. "Can you colour in some eyes?"

"OK!"

"Some of the eyes need to be brown, some blue, some green. I've marked the colours."

"I'll do it t-tomorrow."

"Thanks, Charlie." Matt rubbed his hands. "Right. What do you need?"

"I'm trying to find ssssomeone. She's small, with short red hair and big g-g-g-glasses like this." Charlie sketched the frames with her hands.

"Kat?" said Matt, and Charlie sighed with relief. Matt really did know everyone!

"Can you g-g-give her a note?"

"Sure."

"Th-thanks."

The next day dragged for Charlie. Who knew there could be soooo many hours between eight a.m. and four p.m.?

She helped Dad paint the last bits of the lounge. It was looking really good now! Dad was so happy with it. "Only the hallway left to do now!" he told Charlie. "I reckon, by tomorrow night, we can have our first proper meal at the kitchen table!"

"That's great, Dad."

"Yep," said Dad, looking round the room. "I'm going to miss doing all this when I go back to work." For a moment he stared at his hammer wistfully, and then he said, "Shall we do the bannisters, Charlie?"

Charlie sanded down the bannister rail. She listened to Dad's boring Radio Four programme. But all the time her mind was whirring and her stomach was churning.

Kat was a witch. Did she know? Well, she'd find out soon enough. Charlie pictured the walk to Agatha's cottage. She imagined Agatha leaning in to tell Kat that she was a witch. Charlie threw down her sandpaper. She couldn't bear it! She only knew two people in this stupid village, Kat and Agatha, and now – now they would be in a little club of their own. It would be Kat who got to learn about all the spells and Charlie who ... what? What would she get to do? Pick herbs? Grind stuff up? She felt hollow inside, like a part of her was missing. For a second she hated Kat.

Tick-tock, tick-tock.

The clock was moving so slowly Charlie could have screamed.

She coloured in Matt's homework, filling the brown and blue and green eyes in the faces where Matt had marked them up. Eye colour was genetic, Charlie learned. She made a face as she remembered Agatha saying witch ability sometimes skipped generations. Kat was a very unusual person indeed, Charlie mused, as she coloured.

Tick-tock, tick-tock.

Out of sheer boredom she tidied her room. Her stuff had been in boxes in the wardrobe since they moved in. She upended every box and put her things away: the books on the bookshelf, the ornaments on the chest of drawers. There. Charlie wiped her hands on her jeans; it looked much better.

The clock *finally* moved round to four p.m. Charlie danced from foot to foot in the hall. Matt would be home any second. Hopefully he'd bring Kat's phone number.

Charlie heard the noise of the garden gate. Matt! And he'd brought something better than Kat's number: he'd brought Kat herself. Charlie's stomach dropped. This was it. Kat was about to find out the most amazing thing in the world about herself.

"It's this way." Charlie pointed through the branches.

Kat's glasses wobbled as she nodded. She'd seemed surprisingly laid-back about the whole thing.

Charlie had just said, "Did you m-m-mean what you said? Do you want to h-h-help?"

And Kat had answered simply, "Yes."

She'd looked at Charlie with her bright-green eyes, and Charlie had known, deep down, that Kat could be trusted.

Caw!

The crow danced from one foot to the other on the branch above them.

"Hi, Hopfoot," said Charlie.

He swooped down and circled low over Kat. Then, to Charlie's surprise, he hovered lower until he landed on Kat's shoulder.

"Hello!" she said happily. "Aren't you lovely!" Her Welsh voice grew even softer and more sing-song.

Charlie smiled weakly; they looked like a natural pair: a witch with her pet crow. Hopfoot preened and nibbled Kat's ear, then took flight, leading the way. Charlie sighed inwardly and held the branches open for Kat. Kat bounced through on her tiptoes, darting from side to side to avoid the prickly branches. Charlie crashed through after her. One by one they walked down the narrow path until it opened out on to the clearing.

"Wow!" breathed Kat as she gazed at Agatha's little

tilted cottage. "It's like something from a fairy tale! And it's glowing!"

Charlie tipped her head to the side, puzzled. She couldn't see a glow at all. She still got that warm buzzing feeling, like a quickening in her blood, but nope, no glow. Kat must be really talented.

She knocked at the door. She'd have given anything to be Kat at this moment! She squeezed her hands tight to stop them trembling. Agatha would still let her come over, wouldn't she? All the same, Charlie took care to fix everything in her mind. This might be the last time she walked down the path, the last time she knocked at the cottage door.

She took a deep breath and pushed the door open.

"Well. Come in, come in! Don't stand there all day!" Charlie had never heard Agatha sound so impatient. She swallowed hard and smiled at her friend. Together they stepped into the lounge.

"Whoah!" Kat shielded her eyes. "The glow! It's so bright!" She blinked again and again. Charlie looked from Kat to Agatha, confused. Agatha looked normal to her, but Kat was squinting her eyes up tight.

"Do you see the glow often?" Agatha asked, her eyes sharp.

"No," Kat admitted, "just sometimes. You have it. Suzy at school has it. Charlie has a little glow."

Charlie shifted. "Do I?" She turned her hands over and over, trying to see what Kat was talking about.

"Only now and then. It's very faint."

Charlie frowned.

Agatha came closer. She cupped Kat's face in her hands and stared at her. Kat blinked. "I thought so." The witch stepped back. She smiled. "Haven't seen one like you in a while."

Charlie held her breath. This was it.

"Kat," said Agatha, "have you heard of familiars?"

"Um . . . no," Kat answered, puzzled.

Agatha nodded briskly. Charlie slumped into a chair, her legs weak. Kat perched on the armrest and Charlie felt the crackle of her closeness.

"Familiars help witches," Agatha turned back to explain. "They can make a witch much stronger."

Kat looked puzzled.

"Familiars have their own powers," Agatha went on. "They can draw energy from the earth, from nature." She looked from girl to girl. "Witch and familiar pairings are rare. Some witches never find their familiar. But, if they do, they can achieve great things. Together they are much stronger, much more powerful."

Charlie waited to see what Agatha would say.

"Many familiars are animals. That's why the old tales often feature witches with cats, or toads, or owls, or princes being trapped inside frogs."

Ah. Agatha is talking about Hopfoot. Maybe he'll be Kat's familiar. That's why he was so friendly. Charlie fixed her face so it was blank.

"But once in a while, a human is born a familiar," Agatha continued, "and that's even more special."

Charlie looked up, puzzled. The witch leaned forward. There was a strange tension in the air.

"You, Kat, are a familiar."

Kat jerked and nearly fell off the armrest. Charlie caught her and felt the strange thread of connection. Kat's green eyes were narrowed and her brow was knitted tightly. There was a long silence. Then:

"I thought there was something wrong with me," Kat said. "I mean . . . I can sense things sometimes." Her voice was breathless with the relief of talking about it. "I can feel something under the ground, shifting."

Agatha listened.

"And . . . and animals. They like me. They come to me."

"Yes," Agatha encouraged her.

"I just thought I was weird or . . . or. . ." Kat's voice drifted off, suddenly shy.

"Pah! Weird!" Agatha's voice was sharp. "'Weird' is just another word for 'special'."

Kat nodded slowly. "Is that why I can see the glow?" she asked.

"People experience magic in different ways," said Agatha. "Some see a glow." She looked at Charlie. "Some feel a buzzing."

Charlie nodded. She'd learned to recognize magic now. That weird electrical feeling, like a force was rushing through her. She'd felt it with Agatha and she'd felt it with Kat. And Suzy. And, strangely, the family cottage. She took a breath. *Better get this over with*.

"So," she said, trying to sound casual, "will Kat be your f-f-f-familiar?"

Agatha burst out laughing.

Charlie looked at Kat. Kat shrugged back.

Agatha focused on Charlie's face. "Charlie," she said, "Kat will be *your* familiar."

A sharp thrill gripped Charlie. It ran from her head down to her toes. She hardly dared hope. . .

"You have the gift," Agatha said quickly. "You're a witch." She paused. "Well," she said, waving her hand airily, "you could be, with training."

Charlie's mouth opened and closed. She felt a warmth

135

move up from her belly. A smile washed over her face. She looked at Kat and Kat grinned. But all at once a thought struck her:

"My v-v-v-voice!" Charlie realized. "I can't be a w-witch!"

"Don't be ridiculous!" Agatha spat out. "How many times have I told you there's nothing wrong with your voice! It's perfect for spells."

"Wh-what do you m-mean?"

"Tcha!" Agatha blew through her teeth. "People speak too quickly these days! They don't focus." She pointed her finger straight at Charlie. "For spells you have to feel every letter. Focus on every syllable. Your voice will help you. It'll make you a better witch."

Charlie fell back in the chair. *Her voice would help.*

She'd never, never thought of her stammer as a good thing. It was always a curse, an embarrassment, a shameful bit of her that had to be hidden away. But ... to hear Agatha talk now, her voice might be useful! Happiness bubbled up inside her. She had the gift! Suddenly everything felt good, like her life had slotted into place. She couldn't wait to learn more!

Agatha's brisk voice broke in. "Now," she said, "to business: Suzy."

Charlie felt a rush of panic. Her heart was beating

fast. Now she was a witch it really was her job to stop the curse.

"Together you'll be much stronger," Agatha was saying. "I know you are untrained, Charlie, but with Kat beside you, you can take on a harder spell. And I will help you."

"Do you think I can take off the c-c-curse?"

"Maybe," said Agatha. "The binding said:

'No witch alive can break my spell.'

Charlie – you weren't alive when the spell was cast. Eliza was so cynical about young people it probably never occurred to her that a new witch would come along before Suzy turned seventeen."

"Wh-what do I need to d-d-do?"

"Tell me," the old witch said, spreading her palms wide, "have you heard of a Witch Bottle?"

Charlie's head was spinning. There was so much to take in!

She and Kat had sat in Agatha's cottage till it was dark, hearing all about Witch Bottles and magic and curses. Kat had had to run home to make it by dinnertime.

Now Charlie was in her room, buzzing with the excitement of it all. She was a witch! And she wasn't on her own. Kat would help her. Kat and Agatha.

Witch Bottles were devices to remove curses, Agatha had told them. You put a bit of the victim's hair in the bottle and chanted a spell to suck out the curse. But they could go wrong.

"Be careful," Agatha had warned, waggling her little finger. "A Witch Bottle is powerful magic. If you don't get the spell right then, instead of sucking out the curse, it can steal a bit of you."

Charlie still felt a prickle of fear at that thought.

"It might not work," Agatha had added. "*The proof of the charm is in the spelling.*"

"How will we get Suzy's hair?" Kat had asked.

Charlie's face fell. It was Saturday tomorrow. No school. No chance of bumping into Suzy and pulling off a stray hair.

"You'll need some luck," Agatha had said, and then she'd turned to Charlie. "Do you have any of that white heather left?"

Charlie had nodded. There were a few sprigs left in a jar of water on her window sill.

"Make a little bag out of something personal to you. Fill it with the heather and hang it from your bed. Say:

*'I call on you, oh blessed moon,
I call on you, oh rising sun.
Help me soon,
I cause harm to none.'*

Charlie could hardly sleep from excitement. Her mind turned over and over. The little bag of heather hung from her bedstead. She'd made the bag out of a page of her notebook. It was the most precious thing to her. The page was filled with the table she'd made about witch powers and locations. It made Charlie giggle to think of it now!

She wriggled in bed. No. It was no use. She couldn't sleep. She turned on her light and made a list of all the things she had to do:

Get Suzy's hair. (How? It's Saturday tomorrow, so no school. Go to her house?)
Make Witch Bottle

Agatha had told them they had to design a pattern on the bottle themselves. It had to be the right one to suit the problem.

Charlie chewed her pen and thought about Suzy. She added:

Musical notes?

Suzy had a cat. What was his name? Boots! That was it. What else? Something about the school show? And a witch symbol – a sigil? Soon she had:

Make Witch Bottle. (Musical notes?
Cat? A rainbow? Find right sigil.)

Charlie turned off the light and went to sleep.

Chapter Fifteen

Chop-Chop!

Saturday was bright and sunny. Charlie had arranged to meet Kat at nine a.m., on the edge of town, to see if they could find a way to get Suzy's hair.

"We could sssssearch her bin." Charlie had been thinking about it.

"What if someone sees us?"

"We'll be q-q-quick."

They set off down Wood Street, towards Castle House.

"Eeek!" Kat grabbed Charlie and pulled her behind a tree.

"Whaaa?"

"She's there," Kat said urgently "Look!" She pointed. Suzy was standing on her doorstep, closing her front door.

"Where's she going?" Kat whispered.

They watched as Suzy set off down the street.

"Can you sssneak up on her?" Charlie said in a low voice. "Steal a h-h-hair?"

"I'll try," said Kat. She rocked back and forth on her heels and set off. She was so light on her feet! Charlie watched as she daintily darted just behind Suzy. She was nearly there . . . nearly! Kat reached out her hand. . .

Suzy turned right sharply on to the high street and Kat fell back in disappointment.

They watched as Suzy pushed the door of the first shop. What was it? Charlie followed her to the door, and then spun on her heel and looked at Kat. It was a salon! Suzy had gone to the hairdressers to get a haircut! It was their lucky day! Charlie silently thanked the heather over her bed. Now what. . . ? Her mind made a quick list of possibilities:

Ask the hairdresser for cuttings?
Get a job at the hairdressers?
Walk in and take the hair from the floor?

Then the idea hit her.

"I'll get m-my hair cut too!"

"Can you?" Kat fingered her own short red hair. "I don't think there's much left to come off mine!"

Charlie nodded. Mum would love it. She'd been on at Charlie to get her hair cut for ages. But Charlie worried that the salon looked very posh. She felt in her pocket for money. She had two pounds and Kat had three.

Kat squealed and pointed to a sign that read:

Student training day
Haircuts for £5

Yes!

"You go in!" Kat was practically pushing her. "I'll go to the library and wait. There might be books there about Witch Bottles."

"W-w-wait!" Charlie said in a panic. Going into the salon would mean *talking*: talking to the receptionist *and* the hairdresser.

"What's wrong?"

"M-m-my v-voice."

Kat squeezed her hand. "Remember what Agatha said," she told her friend. "Your stutter is a good thing."

Charlie nodded. She looked through the window at Suzy having her hair washed at the sinks. Her mind made a quick calculation of the number of people in the salon, the fewest words she could get away with using, and how loudly she would have to speak. Then she took a deep breath and pushed the salon door open.

"I-I-I'd like my haircut p-please," she said as confidently as she could.

Charlie's trainee hairdresser was called Fabier and he was very excitable. He bounced up and down as he combed through Charlie's wet hair.

"Eet will be beeeaauuuutiful!" he crooned. He spread a pile of open magazines in front of Charlie and enthusiastically pointed from one picture to another.

To cut down on conversation Charlie just waved her hand over her hair and spluttered out that Fabier could do whatever he wanted. He gave a huge grin, scooped up the magazines and plonked them back on the salon coffee table.

Charlie didn't even look in the mirror. She was far too focused on watching Suzy to care what was happening to her own hair.

Suzy was being snipped just three chairs along. She gave Charlie a little wave and Charlie blushed and glanced down. She could see a nicely trimmed pile of honey-coloured tresses accumulating on the floor under Suzy. One grab and she'd have them. She turned her head sideways to work out the best approach, but was immediately yanked back again by Fabier.

"Don't move!" he snapped "Eet will be *completement* ruined."

Charlie was stuck.

"So you leeeve here in the village?" Fabier asked.

"Um, y-yes. Up by the w-w-woods."

"Ah, *oui*. Little house, like this?" Fabier tipped his palms to the side to mimic the lean of the cottage.

"Yes!" Charlie laughed.

"Ah, that house is old," said Fabier.

"My d-d-dad is rest . . . restoring it," said Charlie.

"Oh, but that is good!" said Fabier. "He is builder?"

"I guess so." Dad kind of *was* a builder these days.

"My friend Daniel, he is starting a beeeeg project on the hill." Fabier picked up the hairdryer and twirled her hair this way and that with a huge round black brush. "He is restoring all the old cottages there."

Charlie's heart picked up. Broom Hill! That's where the witches used to live. They were doing up the old witch cottages! How exciting.

"Daniel, he needs lots of help. There is much work for your dad there, no?"

"Maybe! I'll ask him," Charlie said. He might want another project when their house was done.

Charlie caught a movement from the side. Oh no! Suzy's stylist was nearly finished snipping! In a panic, Charlie suddenly cried out:

"Fabier!"

"What?" He turned off the hairdryer.

". . . um . . . c-c-could I see the sssstyle again? The one in the m-m-m-magazine?"

"Oh yes!" He rushed off all excited to find and show Charlie his source of inspiration.

As soon as he had gone, Charlie crept slowly towards Suzy's chair, keeping low so she didn't notice. She grabbed a handful of hair and shoved it into her pocket.

"Can I help you?" Suzy's stylist asked.

Charlie shook her head, smiled and quickly scurried back to her seat just as Fabier came running up holding the magazine open.

"You will look *très, très belle*!" he cried, resuming his twirling and snipping.

Charlie looked at the page. She had been so busy worrying about Suzy's hair that she'd forgotten about her own. As she looked at the short trendy style in the magazine she gulped. It was all a bit drastic. Her long curly hair was falling to the floor in huge piles. She shut her eyes. Suzy's voice had better be worth all this.

In fact, when it was finished her hair didn't look too

bad. The curls were tamed and organized now. They fell to her shoulders, with little wisps framing her face. Charlie stared at it in the mirror. She looked good.

"You like?" Fabier asked, spreading his hands wide. "No more *Raiponce* ... er ... Rapunzel?"

Charlie smiled at him. "I like!" she said.

She paid her five pounds and rushed to the library, grinning.

"Whoa!" Kat pretended to fall off her seat with shock.

"Very funny," said Charlie.

"It suits you!" said Kat.

Charlie blushed.

"Look what I found!" Kat was holding a page open. "This village is full of witchy stuff!"

Charlie looked around the table. It was covered in books about local history.

Witches of Broomwood.

The Broomwood Witch Trials.

The Sussex Witches.

Kat pointed to a page. There was a photo of a wonky brown bottle. It was made of clay and had marking on its rim. The caption read: BROOMWOOD WITCH BOTTLE, CIRCA 1602.

"That's a W-W-Witch Bottle?"

"Yes. A really old one. I was thinking we could

make ours out of an old glass bottle and paint on some markings. I've copied down the ones on the Broomwood bottle so we can use them for ideas."

Charlie picked up *Witches of Broomwood* and flicked through the pages. It was filled with photographs of women said to be witches. So many of them! She remembered what Agatha had said – one by one they had disappeared, hidden away so as not to be discovered. It was so sad.

She turned a page. There was a photo of a cottage... *Hang on...* Charlie pulled the book closer. The cottage had little stars carved around the chimney. Yes ... it was Charlie's cottage! Puzzled she began to read the caption under the photograph:

WITCH'S COTTAGE, CIRCA 1700.

"What's wrong?" Kat whispered. "You've gone all pale!"

Charlie couldn't speak. She stared dumbly ahead, shaking her head from side to side in disbelief. Her house used to be a witch's cottage! That was why she felt the strange buzzing when she touched its walls.

She looked at the book again and nearly dropped it in shock. The caption carried on in the line below. The whole thing read:

WITCH'S COTTAGE, CIRCA 1700.
SUSPECTED AKELARRE (MEETING PLACE FOR THE
BROOMWOOD COVEN).

Charlie sat down on the floor with a bump.

"What? What is it?" Kat was staring at her.

"That's my house." Charlie pointed at the photo and
Kat leaned in closer.

"Cool! You live in a witch's cottage!"

"Yes but ... but..."

*Agatha... What had she said...? Eliza's cottage used to
be the Akelarre.*

"It's not j-just any cottage. I-I think it-it's Eliza's c-c-
cottage."

"Wow!"

Charlie's mind was a fog of confusion. *Did Great-Aunt
Bess buy it from Eliza? When? How? Eliza was living in it
seventeen years ago, when she put the curse on Suzy. Did Bess
buy it after that?* It didn't make sense.

"I need to ask my mum sssomething," she told Kat.

"OK. Let's go to yours. We can make the bottle there."

Charlie was quiet all the way home, puzzling it
through. She found Mum the second they walked in.
She was sitting on the lounge floor with Annie, building
a tower out of blocks.

"Hello!" Mum looked up in surprise.

"Mum, this is Kat."

"Nice to meet you, Kat. I'm Dawn and this is Annie. Say 'hello', Annie." Annie waved. "But what's happened here?" said Mum, pointing at Charlie's head.

Oh yes! The haircut!

"I love it!" said Mum.

Dad walked in and did a double-take. "You look beautiful, sweetheart!" he said and gave her a big hug. Charlie blushed.

"Thanks. This is Kat."

"Hi, Kat."

"Charlie hair!" cried Annie and Charlie scooped her up.

"Do you like it?" she asked her little sister.

Annie nodded and then, taking advantage of the happy mood, added, "Biscuit?" in a hopeful tone.

Dad laughed and took her. "Come on, Munchkin, we'll find you an apple."

"Mum," Charlie sat down on the rug, "Can you remember anything about B-B-Bess?"

"Who?"

"Great-Aunt Bess. The one you got the c-c-cottage from."

"Let me see... Bess had lived here for years, the

lawyers said. But she didn't have children, so they had to track down her next of kin." Mum frowned. "I don't know exactly how I'm related to her, but it's through my cousin Harry I think. He died years ago so I guess that left me."

"Do you know who Bess b-b-bought the house from?"

"No. But I know she'd lived here for a long time before she died. What is it? You look all puzzled."

Charlie shook her head. "Nothing."

"Well ... I could ask the lawyers more about Elizabeth if you want."

"What?"

"I could ask them about Bess."

"You-you-you said Elizabeth."

"Yes. Bess is short for Elizabeth."

For a moment Charlie's heart stopped beating. Elizabeth. Eliza was short for Elizabeth too. And Eliza had changed her name – Agatha said so.

Charlie glanced at Kat. Her face was drained of colour. Elizabeth. Bess. Eliza. They were the same person. Somewhere down the family line, Eliza was Charlie's relative.

Charlie pulled Kat by the hand. "Thanks, Mum. We're fine. Just off to my room."

*

Upstairs Charlie sat on her bed in shock.

"Eliza is your great-aunt. . ." Kat was repeating it to herself, trying to get her head around it.

Charlie fiddled with the corner of her duvet. "If-if-if my great-aunt p-p-put that curse on," she began hesitantly, "then ssssomewhere, sssomehow, my f-f-family is responsible for what's happened to Suzy." She set her jaw. "I have to fix it."

Kat took her hand. "Let's make this Witch Bottle," she said.

Chapter Sixteen

Practising Witchcraft

They spent the rest of the morning making the Witch Bottle.

Charlie found one of Eliza's old glass bottles, like the one she'd used to put the powder in. It was a little squat one made of clear glass, with a narrow neck and a cork in the top.

Agatha had given Charlie a list of items and they were set out now on a tray on her bed. Every time she added something, Charlie was supposed to focus on the item and what it was meant to do.

Charlie took a deep breath and concentrated hard on the words. "Hair of the victim" – she brushed out Suzy's golden hairs until they shone and put them inside the bottle – "to tempt the c-c-curse in."

"Honey," she said, adding a squeeze, "to make the c-c-curse stick.

"Salt" – she sprinkled a pinch – "to purify."

She pushed the cork in tight.

After lunch the girls took turns to paint markings on the side. They added musical notes, a drawing of a cat and a rainbow. Kat added a sigil she'd seen in the book at the library; it was a kind of wiggly lion inside a jagged circle.

"That's great," said Charlie warmly. "Now let's go!" She was desperate to get to Agatha's. She couldn't wait to tell her about their new discovery!

They hurried through the garden and into the woods.

"Agatha!" Charlie burst into the cottage. "Agatha!"

The witch waved her in. "What happened to your hair?"

Charlie ignored that for the moment. "I l-l-l-live in Eliza's house," she burst out breathlessly.

"I know," said Agatha. "You had one of her bottles for your powder."

"You knew?"

"Yes," Agatha waved her hand. "But it doesn't matter. Someone has to live there."

"No, you-you don't under … understand. There's m-m-m-more." Charlie stopped speaking to draw a long

154

breath in. "Mum got the c-c-c-cottage from my great-aunt. We're her only relatives. Her name was B-B-B-Bess."

It was Agatha's turn to look shocked. She held on to the mantelpiece, her knuckles white. "Eliza was Bess," she said weakly.

Charlie grinned at Kat. She was right! They were the same person.

"She changed her name over and over to hide. She was sometimes Beth, sometimes Lizzie, sometimes Liz and finally Bess."

"Eliza was my great-aunt," said Charlie, "or something like that."

Tears filled Agatha's eyes. "That's wonderful," she said, her voice choked with emotion. She wiped her eyes and forced her voice back to normal. "We can use that link to Eliza. Because you share blood with the curse-giver, you have a better chance of tempting the curse out. Now let's get moving," she said in a rush. "Did you make the bottle? Did you get the hair?"

Charlie pulled the bottle from her pocket. "The h-hair is inside."

Agatha turned the bottle round and round. "I see you have chosen the lion sigil," she said, looking at Kat's painting.

"Yes," said Kat, hesitantly.

"A good choice." Agatha nodded at her. "He represents strength. Now I need you both to concentrate," she continued. "You will need to cast the spell at exactly midnight, and you have to be as close as you can to Suzy."

Charlie and Kat nodded.

"I know where Suzy lives," said Charlie. "We can go to her house."

Agatha continued:

"You each have an important role to play and we only have until tonight to study. This won't be easy. You haven't trained long enough."

Charlie and Kat looked at each other, pale with fright.

"Even so, you are Suzy's only hope." Agatha said firmly. "Together, you'll be more powerful. With both of you, and with your link to Eliza, the Witch Bottle *could* work. But" – Agatha took a deep breath – "it might not. You have to be prepared. If you feel the curse fighting, if the curse starts to come for you, you stop, OK, Charlie? You stop and RUN."

Charlie swallowed hard and nodded. A heavy feeling grew in the pit of her tummy.

*

They practised all afternoon.

Charlie had lines to learn. She had to picture Suzy in her head. Then she had to imagine the curse being pulled out of Suzy.

"That's the most dangerous stage," Agatha warned her. "The curse will be floating around and it won't be contained. Remember," she said, waving her little half-finger, "get it into the bottle as fast as you can."

"How?" Charlie's heart was beating fast at the thought of it.

"You have to draw it in. It won't want to come. It will want to stay with Suzy. You have to picture the hair. Make the curse think the hair is Suzy. Tempt it into the bottle. Then think of the honey. Concentrate until you can almost taste it. Let the honey stick it. When you have it, stopper the bottle."

"What do I do?" Kat asked.

"You need to give Charlie strength. It will be a long time before you properly learn to harness the energy of the earth, but we can try some exercises now. Maybe you'll be able to draw some strength to pass to Charlie. Come."

Agatha led the way outside. The light was beginning to fade and the air had grown misty.

"Sit with me here – you too, Charlie. Take my hands.

Now close your eyes. Empty your mind." Agatha's voice grew soft and rhythmic. "Picture the grass lush and green; picture the soil rich and dark; travel down with me, down under the earth, into the heart of the world. Feel the warmth of the centre, the very core of the world."

Charlie could sense a bit of heat, but Kat gasped and Charlie could feel her friend's hand growing hot.

"I feel it!" Kat cried. "It's glowing all around me."

"Focus on Charlie," said Agatha. "Send the heat to her. Can you do it?"

"I . . . I think so."

Kat's hand tightened and Charlie could feel a gentle warmth spread from her palm across her body. All at once she felt more awake, more alive. The buzzing feeling filled her body with its force, stirring her up inside. Her eyes shot open. "You d-d-did it!" she cried.

"A bit." Kat blushed.

"You will get stronger," Agatha told them. "Both of you. The more you do it, the more powerful you'll become."

Charlie and Kat stayed outside for a long time practising, until it grew too dark to see.

"It's time to go back to your families," said Agatha.

Charlie looked at her watch: it was nearly seven p.m.!

Five hours till midnight! She looked at Agatha anxiously. Agatha put her hands on Charlie's shoulders. "You can do this," she said. "It's meant to be. I feel it."

Charlie nodded.

"Good luck," Agatha whispered. "Blessed be." She mumbled something Charlie didn't catch, and then she leaned in and gave Charlie a kiss on her forehead. "That kiss," she said lightly, "is the first bit of magic I've done in a long time." Agatha tucked her hair behind her ears self-consciously and lifted her hand to wave goodbye.

Charlie and Kat ran back through the woods.

"I'll meet you at eleven-thirty," Kat said, her voice trembling with excitement.

"At the top of Wood Street," Charlie agreed.

Dinner that night was the family's first meal in the new kitchen and everyone wanted to celebrate.

Charlie's mind was dancing around. She couldn't stop picturing what was to come, and her stomach was flip-flopping over and over. She took her place at the table, sitting on her fingers to stop them shaking.

The telephone rang for Dad. A few minutes later he came back, rubbing his head. He sat down hard in his chair. "You know that job I didn't get? The one I went up for London for last week?"

Everyone nodded.

"Well, the guy they chose didn't turn up for work. That was the boss calling me to say they're offering it to me. I start on Monday."

"Hey! That's fantastic!" said Mum.

"Well done, Dad!" said Matt.

Annie banged her spoon.

Charlie smiled. It was the lucky heather! It was making everyone lucky, not just her!

Dad closed his eyes. He didn't look like someone who was having a lucky day.

"What is it?" asked Mum.

"I don't know," Dad said, lifting his head. "I mean, I thought I wanted to go back to computer programming. I thought I was desperate to get that job. But..." He waved his hand around the kitchen. "I've loved doing up this house," he said, "and I can't bear the thought of going back to work!"

There was a long silence. Then Mum said, "Darling, you should do what you want to do."

"But how can we afford it?" Dad said in despair. "I'll never find a job as a builder!"

"Wait!" It came back to Charlie in a flash. "They're d-d-doing up the old c-c-cottages on Broom Hill," she said. "You could get a job there!"

Dad lifted his eyebrows, "Maybe I could..." he said slowly.

"And, you know," Mum added, "I'm really enjoying my job."

"Are you?"

"Yes! I felt bad about saying it while you couldn't find a job of your own, but," she confessed, "I love it!"

Dad gave a broad grin. "Then I'm not going back to computing!" he said, his eyes shining with excitement. "I'll ask about a job on the Broom Hill project and, even if I don't get that, something will come along. I'm feeling lucky!"

"We've all got something to celebrate then," said Mum, raising a glass. "Matt's finally finished that science project."

"Did the last bit today!" said Matt, mouthing his thanks at Charlie.

"Charlie's made a new friend," Dad continued. She was pleased he'd glossed over the whole candle/exclusion thing.

"And Annie's wearing big-girl pants," said Mum.

In her highchair, Annie pulled up her dress to show Charlie.

"Th-that's great, Annie!" she said.

"Princess pants," said Annie, pointing at Snow White.

161

"I sssee!" Charlie stroked her sister's hair and grinned. Dad would be a builder. Mum would carry on being a nurse and their daughter would be a witch. Well, if she could get this spell to work tonight.

And if she didn't get injured in the process.

Chapter Seventeen

How to Catch a Witch

At eleven o'clock Charlie pulled her covers back and slid out of bed. She was still wearing the jeans and top she'd had on earlier and she tied her shoelaces as quickly as she could.

In her bag were:

One torch.

One Witch Bottle.

One piece of notepaper with the words of the spell.

One bandage (just in case).

Charlie gave a shiver as she pictured Agatha's little finger.

She opened her door, tiptoed across the hall and down the stairs. She closed the front door slowly behind her, turning the catch gently so it didn't bang. She'd left a note for Mum and Dad on her desk in case they noticed she was out. It just said:

Gone for a midnight walk with Kat.

She waved to Hopfoot, who was sitting on the wall. As soon as he saw her, he took off and circled above her. Charlie smiled. It was good to have company.

As she walked, she remembered what Agatha had said about drawing the curse out. "It's like tug of war," were her words. What would it feel like? She'd practised saying the chant over and over, but she had no idea what would happen when she actually used it. Would she be able to control the curse? Tempt it into the bottle?

Charlie clenched her fists. Tonight she'd find out whether Agatha was right: whether she really did have the gift.

"Hey!" Kat whispered to her from the start of Wood Street. She was bouncing on her tiptoes, desperate to get going.

"Hi!" Charlie giggled in excitement.

They linked arms and walked up the road as quietly as they could. Their footsteps echoed on the concrete as they crept past the sleeping houses.

Soon they reached Castle House. It looked like a real castle in the moonlight, the turrets casting strange, eerie shadows across the ground. Hopfoot flew up and landed on the roof.

"That's Suzy's w-w-window," Charlie said under her breath. She pointed to where she'd seen Suzy singing two weeks earlier.

"How do we get closer?" Kat whispered back. She wiggled a drainpipe and it groaned.

Both girls froze.

"Sorry," Kat murmured.

There was a *Caw!* and Hopfoot swooped down and landed in the side passage. Charlie crept along the side of the house after the crow. He was perched on top of a ladder.

"Clever you," Charlie whispered, and Hopfoot lifted his black head higher.

Together, Charlie and Kat carried the ladder over to Suzy's window. Charlie crossed her fingers that no one would walk past and ask them what they were doing! Hopfoot flew up to the turret as if to keep watch.

Carefully they placed the ladder against the wall. Charlie's heart was beating so fast it was threatening to burst out of her chest. She looked at her watch: ten to midnight. It was nearly time. She could feel her tongue growing thick and her throat closing up at the thought of chanting the spell. She swallowed again and again, but it still felt like her mouth was filled with cotton wool.

Kat took a flask out of her bag. "It's lemon tea," she said. "Agatha said it would help."

Charlie smiled at her gratefully and took a sip. The warm liquid ran down the back of her throat and she felt the blockage easing. She took a deep breath in and out. Her voice was an asset. It would help her focus, she told herself.

Charlie pulled out the Witch Bottle, turning it over and over in her hands. Kat sat on the grass at the bottom of the ladder and closed her eyes as Agatha had showed her. Her brow furrowed in concentration as she tried to draw out energy from under the ground.

At exactly five to midnight, Charlie tucked the bottle back into her jacket pocket and slowly climbed the ladder to Suzy's window, trying not to creak on every step. She held herself in place just outside the glass and peered in between a crack in the curtains. The room was dark, but Charlie could make out Suzy's shape in the bed. The clouds lifted and the full moon shot a narrow dart of white light into the room. Charlie could see Suzy's face, troubled even in sleep. A low tingle ran up from her tummy. It was the curse, buzzing and dancing.

Charlie steadied herself and closed her eyes to focus. She pictured the words she needed, imagining every letter, every syllable. In an even voice she began to chant:

"By midnight clear,
By starlight strong,
I call you near,
Heed my song."

A hiss filled her ears. She could feel something shifting. The air went cold and Charlie shivered. The curse was waking!

A wisp of bright green rose from the bed. And another. And another. The wisps spun and gathered, twisting and plaiting themselves to form a rope of cold green fire. The rope wound itself around Suzy, binding her tight in a python grip.

The crackle in the air grew louder and the buzzing felt worse than ever: a harsh scratching, rubbing at the inside of Charlie's bones. Her hands trembled. She bit her lip hard and concentrated on pulling the end of the rope. She pictured the words she needed:

"Untie! Be free!
Relax! Release!
Let Suzy be,
Leave her in peace!"

The rope began to uncoil from the body on the bed.

This was the most dangerous part, Agatha had said. The curse was free! It floated upright just above the bed, swaying back and forth like a hypnotized snake.

Charlie steeled herself ready. She had to tame it, and she had to be fast. There was no time to worry about speaking. No time to do anything other than focus on the letters.

"I'm of the kin,
I share Eliza's line,
I call you in,
I declare you mine."

Now she knew what Agatha meant: it *was* like tug of war. The curse wanted to dive back down into Suzy. Charlie could feel it pulling to get away, to return to the body it came from. In her mind, Charlie pulled and pulled at the end of the long rope. It was so tiring! For a second her concentration dropped and she nearly lost her balance on the ladder. The curse fell away from her. She gave a little shriek as it slipped and flailed from wall to wall, flicking green sparks across the room. Charlie ducked as a finger of icy flame rushed at her. She'd lost control! Her legs tensed, ready to run.

All at once a warm force hit her from below. It was Kat! At the bottom of the ladder the familiar was sending up energy. Charlie breathed in hard and tightened her grip on the ladder. With Kat's help she felt braver. She set her shoulders and focused on the rope of cold flame. She pictured Suzy's hair, trying to trick the curse that Suzy was in the bottle. She said the words again, stronger this time. Her voice rang out clear and true:

*"I call you in,
I declare you mine!"*

She yanked hard in her mind, wrenching the rope, tugging it towards her.

The curse was confused, she could feel it. It pulled this way and that, first to the bottle then to the figure on the bed. Charlie centred herself, fixing the image of Suzy's golden hair in her mind.

Whoosh!

The curse shot straight towards Charlie. The air was filled with a freezing green smoke that chilled her to the bone. She held out the bottle and the evil vapour curled itself in.

Charlie thought of the honey now, sticking the curse into place. She imagined tasting it, feeling the sweet gloopiness clogging her throat and trapping the curse.

"Light of light,
Sweet of sweet,
Bind it tight,
The spell's complete."

She fumbled with the cork. *Hurry! Hurry!* she told her shaking fingers. *There!* She pushed it down hard.

She had it! She had caught the curse.

Charlie heard a soft sigh from the bed. Suzy rolled over. A smile spread across her face as she snuggled down under her duvet, peaceful at last.

Charlie's knees trembled in relief.

The ladder wobbled as she staggered down rung by rung and fell to the floor.

"What happened? Are you all right?" Charlie could hear the worry in Kat's voice.

"I-I'm OK," she answered feebly. She was exhausted!

"Did you get it?" Kat whispered anxiously.

Charlie lifted her tired head and grinned at her. "Got it!" she said. She lifted up the bottle for Kat to see.

Together they peered at the swirling mass of green smoke. With a shaky finger Kat reached out and touched the Witch Bottle.

"It feels so cold," she said, yanking her finger back.

Charlie shivered. "Let's take it to Agatha," she said. "I can't wait to get rid of it."

Kat put the ladder away then she gave her arm to Charlie. Together they stumbled down Wood Street as quick as they could. Hopfoot was faster, flitting in and out of the trees.

As soon as they were out of the village, Charlie and Kat whooped for joy.

"We did it!" they cried as, arms entwined, they lurched through the woods and toppled through the cottage door.

Agatha was waiting for them. She turned pale when she saw Charlie leaning on Kat.

"What happened?" she asked quickly.

"I'm fine!" Charlie laughed, and fell on to an armchair. "My l-l-legs are just a bit wobbly."

She reached into her pocket and held up the Witch Bottle in triumph.

A quick smile spread across Agatha's face. She took the bottle from Charlie and cradled it in her hands. "Eliza's curse," she said in a low, soft voice.

Charlie and Kat looked at each other but stayed silent.

Agatha sighed. Her knuckles turned white as she squeezed the Witch Bottle. The green smoke swirled up to meet her fingers, pushing angrily against the inside of the glass. "This was what finally did it." Her voice turned sharp. "This brought the havoc, and her death." She turned to the fire. "Stand back!" she shouted.

Charlie and Kat drew back to the doorway as Agatha lifted her arm. She threw the bottle hard into the fire. There was a flash of green and a loud hiss as the glass bottle exploded.

When Charlie lifted her head she found Agatha looking at her.

"It is done," said Agatha, her voice calmer.

But there was something Charlie had to know.

"If I'm related to Eliza, d-does that mean I'm ... b-b-bad?"

Agatha stepped forward and took Charlie's face in her hands. "No," she said softly. "It is our actions that decide whether we are good or bad. Eliza wasn't bad inside, she just chose the wrong path." Her purple eyes were bright. "You did well, Charlie. I'm proud of you," she said. "Both of you."

Charlie felt a weight lift off her shoulders. "Thank you for t-t-teaching me," she said.

Agatha cleared her throat and stood back. "Right. That's enough fun. We've got lots to do. *Spells don't charm themselves.*"

"Um," Kat said, raising her hand sleepily, "it's the middle of the night."

Charlie yawned.

"Oh, yes," Agatha realized. "Yes it is. Right. Well, tomorrow then? And the next day too. I think we'll start with sigils ... no ... with telepathy. That will be most useful." Her eyes shone with excitement.

Charlie and Kat looked at one another and grinned.

Sleepily they said goodbye to Agatha.

"See you t-t-tomorrow." Charlie waved as they left the witch in the doorway, still thinking through plans.

The girls parted at the old apple tree. "I've got to get back before Mum wakes up," Kat said.

Charlie hugged her. "Thank you." She was so pleased to have someone to share this adventure with!

Charlie stumbled home, tripping over her feet from exhaustion. She fell into bed, hoping for a few hours' sleep before the family woke up. Her mind was still spinning from everything she'd seen that evening. They had done it! Suzy was free! She could sing in the school show on Monday. Charlie would watch her skipping down the Yellow Brick Road, knowing it had been the two of them – Charlie and Kat, witch and familiar – who had saved her.

She felt a little flip in her tummy at the thought of school. Heat filled her cheeks as she remembered the small matter of nearly setting fire to the music room. Then she swallowed. She was a witch now. Like Agatha had said, the path she'd chosen wouldn't be an easy one. *But I can do it*, Charlie whispered to herself.

She touched the cottage wall and felt the usual buzz. It didn't frighten her anymore. It was her connection with magic, with Eliza. Charlie gave secret thanks to her long-lost aunt for passing on the magic gene, even if Eliza had made mistakes at the end.

She thought back to when she'd first arrived, how she'd believed there was a vampire or a ghost living in the walls. She'd hated her voice so much during those first few weeks, starting her new school. Now . . . well, it was annoying sometimes, but it was worth putting up with. It would make her a better witch, Agatha said.

Charlie grinned as she remembered the list she'd made:

Ways to Catch a witch,

she'd called it. Now, in her head she added:

Number 7: Look in the mirror

Read on for a sneak peek at
Charlie's next magical adventure:

How to
Trap a
Wolf

Chapter One

"Again!" commanded the witch. She stamped her foot, and the ragged hem of her black dress swished across the muddy earth.

"Again? Really?" Charlie wriggled to find a more comfy position. It was getting chilly out here in the woods. The autumn leaves were scratchy under her jeans and her legs were starting to cramp.

"It's cold," her friend Kat grumbled opposite her. With her eyes closed, Charlie made a sympathetic face in response.

The witch sighed. "All right. Let's stop for a bit. Come back in and we'll have tea." She turned on the heel of her black boot and opened the door of her tumbled-down cottage.

Charlie let out a breath of relief. She opened her eyes to find Kat grinning.

"Thought she'd never give us a rest!" Kat's eyes flashed bright green under her huge glasses.

"I kn-know! We've been out here for hours!" Charlie shook out her aching limbs and turned her face to the weak sun.

Agatha was a hard taskmaster. For the last seven months the witch had been pushing Charlie and Kat further and further, helping them to develop their magical powers. It wasn't easy. Spells took a lot of practice. And there was so much to learn.

Charlie scribbled a quick note in the lever-arch file next to her:

Wear warmer clothes for telepathy lessons.

The file was now so full of information it needed coloured dividers for all the sections. Charlie flipped the pages back to the start, feeling the heavy weight of her work – all that writing! She'd even had to make a contents page to organize it. She ran her finger over the biro indents:

Herbs:
Healing
Luck
Protection
Energy
Love/Friendship
Sleep

Crystals:
Healing
Prophesy
Communication
Calming

Charlie stopped her finger at:

Moon Phases:
New
Waxing
Full
Waning
Eclipse

She felt a thrill run down her spine. There was due to be an eclipse in three weeks' time. Everyone in town was talking about it. What's more, it would be on the 31st October: Halloween (or "Samhain" as Agatha called it).

Samhain marked the end of summer and the start of the colder, harder months. It was an important night for witches. Traditionally, the Samhain blessing they chanted brought luck and strength to the village to see the people through the winter ahead. In Broomwood, Charlie's village, no one had done the blessing for seventeen years; not since Agatha had given up magic. The winters had felt long and harsh. Some of the houses had been flooded at Christmas time three years in a row.

This year, Charlie was determined things would be different. Agatha had said that, if they were ready, Charlie and Kat could do the Samhain ritual themselves! Charlie grinned to herself – she couldn't wait. When an eclipse fell, when the moon was dark, witchcraft was at its most powerful. Their magic would be extra strong. Charlie glanced at her note:

Eclipse + Samhain = Something Special

Three weeks to go … then Charlie and Kat would do their first blessing! Maybe it would bring the village good luck.

A low buzzing ran through Charlie's bones at the thought of it, making her squirm.

"Whoah!" cried Kat, "You're glowing so brightly!" she shielded her eyes with her hand.

"Sorry!" laughed Charlie. "I was just th-thinking about Halloween."

"Well stop it or I'll have to get prescription sunglasses."

Kat sensed magic by light. To her, Agatha and Charlie had a soft glow. Whenever the two witches were doing a spell, the glow became stronger. For Charlie, magic felt like the warm fizz of electrical current. She forced her mind away from Halloween and the buzzing in her bones eased.

"Tea's ready!" called Agatha from the cottage.

Kat sprang to her feet. She held out her hand to pull Charlie up and, as they touched, Charlie felt the hum of connection between them. Charlie was a new witch and Kat was her familiar. Familiars were usually animals: toads or crows, or cats. But Kat was a human familiar and together, Agatha had told them, Charlie and Kat could be very powerful.

Charlie pushed open the door of Agatha's old cottage. The air was steamy and a pot of water bubbled on the fire. Charlie ducked under a hanging crystal and plonked herself on the rug by the flames. She rubbed her hands to warm them and Agatha passed her a mug of hot tea.

Charlie bent her head and breathed in the steam; it smelled sweet and spicy. She looked up to find Agatha raising her eyebrows in a silent question.

"OK," Charlie sighed. She sniffed the tea. "Um … I can smell h-h-honey…" She sniffed again. "Chamomile, lavender…" She screwed up her face to try and identify the other herbs. There was something sharper there too…"N-nettle?" she tried.

Agatha gave a little nod.

Phew. Little nods counted as high praise from Agatha.

"For energy," Agatha explained as she gave Kat a mug of her own.

Charlie nursed the hot mug in her hands, warming her fingers. She took a little sip and gave a shiver of pleasure as the warm liquid ran through her.

Kat looked at her watch. "Whoops! It's five – I have to be getting back soon," she said. "Mum'll be home from work in an hour." Kat's mum worked shifts at the local supermarket.

Five p.m.! Charlie was shocked too. Where had the day gone? Oh yes: mainly sitting on the cold ground, failing at telepathy. She rubbed the base of her back.

"Do you think we'll ever be able to see into each other's heads?"

"You will," answered Agatha firmly. "You just have to focus."

"I am f-f-focusing," muttered Charlie defensively. She blushed as she felt her stammer flare up.

"No – you're thinking. I can tell." Agatha pursed her mouth. "It's not something you can force, Charlie. You have to feel it." Agatha put her gloved hand on the top of Charlie's head and a warm tingle ran across her scalp.

"Relax your body." Agatha's voice became low and soft. "Concentrate on your breathing. Feel the air flowing into your body and out again. Let your mind go."

Charlie could hear the gentle crackle of the fire; she felt the warmth of the rug under her legs. Her limbs softened and her head dropped under Agatha's hand.

"Try to keep your thoughts still," said the witch softly. "Focus on one thing."

Charlie felt sleepy. She pictured her nice warm bed, her duvet pulled up tight to her shoulders and her pouch of lucky heather swinging over her head, back and forth, back and forth. She could smell a sweet, woody fragrance and a memory popped into her head. All at once she was back there, on the moonlit heath. A little white plant sparkled brightly before her and Hopfoot the crow was cawing in her ear as she snipped a flower.

Kat gave a cry and Charlie opened her eyes.

"I saw it! Just for a second, but I saw it!" The familiar was nodding in excitement, her glasses jiggling up and down wildly on her nose. "You were on open land somewhere, and there was a white flower."

Charlie's face broke into a wide grin. "I was p-picking heather!" she said. She looked at Agatha, her eyes bright.

Agatha gave a little nod as she took her hand away from Charlie's head.

"I'm home!" Charlie's voice rang out in the hallway. She heard a muffled response from the top of the house, and made her way up the teeny cottage stairs to see Mum poking her head upside down from a hatch in the ceiling.

"We're clearing out the loft," Mum announced. There was a tinkle of metal and Mum pulled her head back up for a moment. "No, Annie! Put that down," she yelled to Charlie's little sister. Then she was back. "There's all kinds of junk up here. It's a real mess – Annie's having a great time. Come and see!"

Charlie put a foot on the ladder to climb up, and felt a shiver of electricity run through her. The family had inherited their house from Mum's distant relative, Great Aunt Bess. Mum and Dad loved the old cottage, with its wonky stairs and ancient stone walls. They had no idea that, when Bess was alive:

1. She was sometimes known as Eliza
2. She was a friend of Agatha's and, most importantly…
3. She was a witch

Not only a witch, but a witch who had got herself tangled in some very dark magic. Charlie frowned. She hoped there wasn't anything too dangerous hiding up there in the loft.

Charlie pulled herself up onto the old dusty floor and gazed around. Wow. Mum wasn't joking – the attic was a mess! There were old saucepans, and bundles of fabric. Ancient leather suitcases were piled in the corner with cracked plates teetering precariously on top of them, and under the eaves an armchair lay on its side, with its springs popping out. Annie was jumping up and down on a worn out sofa cushion, sending up puffs of dust into the air with a "Wheee!"

Mum was twirling around in an old hat and a set of pearls.

"Ta-da!" she said, waving her arms high. "I found a whole box of clothes and scarves. Some of them are gorgeous!"

"What's it all doing up here?"

"Everything Bess owned got stored up here in case we

wanted it." Mum waved her hand around the space. "I think most of it's rubbish but there could be a few pieces of interest. dad might know."

Charlie's Dad was working on a big restoration project out at Broom Hill on the edge of town. He was becoming an expert in old property and possessions. Every now and then he came home raving about a bit of ancient kitchen equipment or jewellery he'd dug up and handed in to Broomwood Museum.

Charlie sifted through the wooden crates. There didn't seem to be anything witch-like. There were no potions or bottles or jars of herbs. Agatha had said Great-Aunt Bess had become very strange in the years before she died; she'd found an old grimoire, a book of dark magic called *The Book of Shadows*. She grew obsessed with dark magic – and it had ended in disaster. Charlie's eyes flicked around the room but could see nothing ominous. Bess must have either got rid of anything magic-related before she died, or else she had kept it all somewhere else.

Idly Charlie opened another wooden crate and a quickening rushed through her blood. Her fingers prickled and her scalp started to tingle. She had spoken too soon; there was something magic here! Charlie glanced at Mum – who was busy trying to rescue Annie from a pile of dusty sheets she'd wrapped herself in – and then eased her fingers down into the crate. The tingling came from something at the bottom. It was tugging at her attention, calling her hand down to find it. Her fingers closed around something cold and hard. She drew it up in her fist and nervously opened her hand.

There on her palm sat a grey stone ladybird, with spots carved into its back. It was heavy and smooth, around the size of a yo-yo. A shallow split ran across the top, dividing the stone into two wings. Charlie ran her fingers along the crack. She tilted the ladybird and heard a slight rattle. She shook it and heard the sound again. There was something inside! With her back to Mum, Charlie tried to open the ladybird, first twisting it, then pushing her fingers into the narrow split. The stone refused to move. Maybe it wasn't supposed to open? Maybe it was sealed fast? No. There was something special about this stone, Charlie was sure – something inside it. She just needed longer to figure it out. She squeezed it into the back pocket of her jeans.

"I'm going back d-down," she said, with her feet on the ladder. "I need to get my things r-ready for school tomorrow."

"Oh cripes! It's getting late! I hadn't noticed," cried Mum. She pulled off the hat. "And Annie, you're filthy!" Clouds of grey puffed out of Annie's clothes. Annie grinned proudly as if this was the best news ever. "I didn't realize the time! I haven't even started cooking!"

"Don't worry!" Dad called from downstairs. "I'm home now and I've got the dinner on."

"Thanks, love!" Mum called back. "Here, you take Annie." She handed the little girl to Charlie and then followed them down the ladder, a box of old scarves on her hip.

As they stared at each other in the hallway Charlie had to laugh. Annie wasn't the only one messy from the attic. Mum had a cobweb in her hair and a streak of something greyish across her cheek.

"Go and have a sh-shower, Mum," said Charlie. "I'll put Annie in the bath."

Mum gave her a dusty kiss.

"Come on, Annie," Charlie said, jiggling her sister on her hip. "Let's get you cleaned up."

"Bubbles?" Annie's voice was hopeful.

"Of course! We can p-pop them together." Charlie put one finger in her cheek and pulled it out, Pop! Annie laughed.

"Again! Again!"

"You'll be sorry you started that trick," Mum groaned as she headed towards her shower room. "She'll make you do it over and over."

"Again! Again!"

*

That night in her room Charlie sat at her desk, turning the stone ladybird around in her hands. She shook it and heard the rattle.

"What are you hiding?" Charlie whispered.

A gust of wind blew in through Charlie's open window and her papers flew across her desk. Charlie jumped up to rescue them. She closed her window and put the ladybird down as a paperweight.

There it sat on her desk, silently waiting.

Chapter Two

Mum gave Charlie and Matt a lift to school the next morning.

"I've got rehearsal after school," Matt reminded Mum, as they climbed out of the car, "so I'll be home late." Charlie's brother was in the school production of Macbeth. He was playing one of the witches.

"I'll be late as well," Charlie added. "I'm hanging out with Kat." It wasn't a total lie. She would be with Kat; it's just that Agatha would be there too, and they would be practising magic. "Have a good d-day at work," she said, waving goodbye to Mum.

"Bye, Annie!" Matt blew her a kiss. "Have fun at nursery!"

Kat was waiting for Charlie in their usual spot, just

outside the school entrance. Today she wore bright stripy green-and-pink tights. Charlie grinned and shook her head. Kat was always in trouble for breaking the school uniform rules but she didn't seem to care. She did her lunchtime detentions quite cheerfully and continued to wear her crazy tights.

"How are you?" she asked. "Anything exciting happen last night?"

"Actually, it d-did. I found something c-cool!" Charlie dropped her voice to a whisper as Matt walked past them into school. "It belonged to Eliza – I found it in the attic – and there's something m-m-magic about it, I can tell!"

Kat's eyes widened.

"I know!" Charlie said. "It c-could be really exciting!" It took her a second to realize that Kat wasn't paying her any attention at all. Instead, she was staring at something behind Charlie.

Charlie turned around.

An older boy was riding down the drive, standing upright on the side of his bike with both feet on the same pedal. He had a wide grin on his face and the glint of a silver earring in one ear. His hair flopped over his eyes and he lifted a hand casually to sweep it back. The bike leaned as he looped lazily from one side of the drive to the other.

A Year 13 girl with spiky hair was riding just ahead of him, heading for the last space on the bike rack. The boy narrowed his eyes, flung his right leg over the bike seat and pedalled hard straight towards it. With a screech of his brakes, he swooped into the final bike slot just in front of Spiky.

"Hey!" She looked up. "That was my space."

"Sorry," said the boy flippantly, in a broad Northern accent. "I got here first." He locked up his bike and strolled passed Charlie and Kat into the school office.

"Who is that?" Kat turned to Charlie.

"I don't know," said Charlie irritably. "He m-must be new… Did you hear w-what I was saying before?"

"Oh. Sorry. What?" Kat said.

"Never m-m-mind," mumbled Charlie as they walked through the entrance.

The boy was just ahead of them, approaching the reception office. He knocked on the side of the glass hatch. "Zak Crawford, Year 9," he drawled.

"Hello!" Mrs Fisher in the school office gave him a welcoming smile. "If you wait on the sofa for a moment, a buddy from your year will come to collect you."

"What?" said Zak, "I don't need a buddy," he emphasized the word as if it was the stupidest thing in the world.

Charlie walked on past Zak towards the double doors

that led to the hallway. She turned to roll her eyes at Kat but her friend wasn't there. Charlie looked back to see Kat pretending to tie her shoelace, just by the new boy.

Mrs Fisher was still explaining the merits of the buddy system to Zak. "They'll help you find your way around, introduce you to friends…"

"I don't think I'll need help making friends," Zak sneered. "I'll just try my luck. Without a buddy."

"Wait!" Mrs Fisher called after him. "Hang on … there are some papers … ah…" She leaned out of the hatch but he ignored her and strode past Charlie to the double doors, marching through them and not caring that they swung back and nearly hit her.

"Nice," said Charlie sarcastically.

"Yep," said Kat as she caught up. "I'm glad I stayed to check him out. At least we know what he's like now. He might be cute, but he's not likely to make friends with that attitude." She waved to Charlie as the bell rang. "See you for lunch later."

By break time it was clear that Charlie and Kat weren't the only ones to find Zak annoying. According to school gossip, in PE he'd refused to pass the football even once, in music he'd carried on a long drum solo drowning out the guitar riff Toby had been practising for ages, and in art he'd sniggered at Katie's self-portrait.

He was certainly causing a stir. Throughout the morning Charlie heard rumour after rumour:

Zak had been expelled from his last school.

His parents had sent him away to live with his grandparents.

He was mean.

He was a show-off.

His trouser legs were too short.

He was Bad News.

At lunch, Charlie took her tray and joined Kat at their favourite table.

"Water?" Kat said, holding up a jug.

Charlie nodded. Kat poured it into Charlie's glass. Just as she lifted it to her lips, Charlie caught a sharp smell, like vinegar.

"Ew," she wrinkled her nose and put her glass down again.

"What?" Kat looked puzzled. She took a swig of her own water. "It's fine!" she said, shrugging. "It's just water."

Charlie sniffed hers again and pushed it aside. It smelt awful – the school must be using some new filter. No one else seemed bothered – all around her children were gulping it down – but just the smell of it made her retch. She made a mental note to bring in her own water bottle from now on.

"Don't look," Kat said in a whisper. Charlie looked. Zak had walked in.

"I said don't look!"

"Sorry!" Charlie looked back down.

Kat's green eyes followed Zak.

"You know," she said, as she sipped her water, "maybe we're being a bit harsh. Maybe he's just nervous." She took another sip. "He seems quite nice, actually."

"You've never even sp-spoken to him," said Charlie dismissively.

"No, but there's something about him… I can't put my finger on it…"

Charlie felt a little shiver of jealousy run through her as she watched her friend gazing across the canteen, her eyes fixed on the new boy.

It wasn't just Kat who seemed to be warming to Zak. At the end of school that day a handful of students had gathered by his locker.

"Hey, nice ball work in PE," Kevin Anders said, high-fiving him.

Toby gave Zak a nod of appreciation. "Cool drums, man."

Charlie kept walking. There was no way she was giving Zak any attention.

"Wa-ha ha ha!" She heard a loud cackle from the school hall and poked her head through the doorway. The rehearsal for Macbeth was in full swing. Charlie saw Matt standing in a group of three.

"When shall we three meet again?" one actor read from her script.

"You need to sound more witch-like, Janine," came Miss Knevitt's voice from the director's chair. "Witches are old hags."

Charlie bit back a smile.

Janine hunched her back. She scowled and made her voice shaky.

"When shall we three meet again?" she rasped, sounding like a strangled cat.

"Perfect!" cried Miss Knevitt. "You sound exactly right. Just like a witch."

To Charlie's amazement, over the next few days, Zak somehow became more and more popular. To Charlie it seemed he was no less annoying, no less arrogant, no less Bad News. But it soon became clear that the rest of the school saw things differently.

Even Kat had taken to lingering for longer and longer

periods of time by the school exit. Every day Charlie felt like she was practically dragging her friend to Agatha's.

"Just a minute," Kat would say, adjusting her glasses casually as she scanned every student leaving. "You start. I'll catch you up!"

And every day Charlie would head off on her own.

By Friday morning, in the eyes of the school, Zak had turned into some kind of mini-god and Kat could talk about nothing else. Charlie was completely fed up.

Then, that lunchtime, Suzy Evans, the coolest girl in school, invited Zak Crawford on to the Year 12 and 13 canteen table next to the window. This was the greatest honour that had ever been bestowed on a Year 9.

That Friday afternoon, on the way to Agatha's, Kat was still talking about Zak. She bounced through the woods, chattering away;

"Did you notice he has a little scar just by his mouth? I wonder how he got that."

Charlie shrugged in answer as she snapped a skinny branch off a nearby bush and broke it apart in her fingers. Kat was her friend. Her only friend, if she was honest. And they were supposed to be a team, just the two of them.

There was a loud *Caw!* from a treetop and a crow

swooped down. "Oh, hi, Hopfoot!" said Kat happily as he perched on her shoulder. She tickled the top of his head and he ruffled his feathers against her.

"Hi," said Charlie, but Hopfoot ignored her and cuddled into Kat's neck.

Grumpily, Charlie left them behind and pushed through the bushes to find the narrow path to Agatha's house. There was a fine drizzle in the air and the branches pinged back against her, showering little splashes on to her face. In frustration Charlie shoved one bush hard and scratched her hand on a bramble. She stomped into the cottage.

"Who put a curse in your bonnet?" the witch asked as Charlie slumped down in an armchair. Agatha raised her eyebrows but Charlie shook her head. She didn't want to talk about it.

Kat came in, Hopfoot on her shoulder.

"I think someone's hungry," she laughed as the crow nibbled the ends of her short red hair. "Ow! Hopfoot! Leave some hair for me!"

Agatha handed her some nuts and Hopfoot happily munched them out of Kat's palm.

"Right," the old witch began. "We've got just over two weeks until Samhain and, if you're going to do the blessing together, there's still a lot of work to do." Charlie winced. Despite trying every day, they hadn't managed to repeat their telepathy skills of last Sunday night.

Charlie took her place on the rug opposite Kat and crossed her legs under her knees.

"Now," said Agatha, "empty your minds. Focus on your breathing. Slow down. Feel the air flow in and out…"

There was an itch on Charlie's neck. One of her curls was caught under her collar and it tickled against her skin. Should she brush it away? If she did then Agatha would know she wasn't concentrating. But if she didn't it was going to annoy her. Would that be worse? Maybe, if Agatha wasn't watching, she could sneak her hand up. She opened her eyes a tiny bit. All she could see was the old rug on the floor. Her face was still wet from the drizzle and her jumper felt heavy and damp on her shoulders. She shifted slightly to ease the itch.

"Stop," said Agatha, and Charlie opened her eyes. The witch was looking at her closely.

"S-s-sorry," Charlie mumbled. She pulled her hair out of her shirt collar.

Kat blinked and yawned. She looked like she was waking from a trance. At least one of them had got it right.

"Let's try something else for now," said Agatha. She

lifted a pile of long thin twigs. "You can help me make a blessing wreath for the new year."

"New year?"

"Yes. Samhain – what you call Halloween. The new year."

Charlie looked at Kat, confused. Surely New Year was January the first? Kat shrugged in answer.

"January isn't the new year for witches," said Agatha quickly, as if she'd read Charlie's thoughts. "Our calendar starts on November 1st. Remember I told you Samhain marks the end of the harvest and the start of the cold weather? That's why we do the blessing then, on the night of 31st October. We give thanks for the old year past, and we wish for peace for the new year to come." She lifted the twigs on to her lap and began to plait. Her gloved fingers moved quickly over and under and soon she had the start of a circular shape.

Charlie curled her feet to the side and picked up some twigs of her own. They were thin and bendy – they looked like they were made from an old vine.

"Honeysuckle," said Agatha in answer to Charlie's unasked question. "It aids friendship," she added quickly and reached for another twig. Charlie sneaked a glance at Kat, but her friend was absorbed in her task, weaving the twigs in and out.

Charlie looked down. There was silence for a while. Charlie concentrated on plaiting. After a time, Agatha spoke again.

"Eliza and I used to make these together," she said. "We sat right here, by the fire, years ago." The witch reached for another twig and paused a moment before she plaited it in. "Eliza loved Samhain!" she said with a little smile. "She would write a new blessing chant every year for us to say."

"Can witches write their own sp-spells?" Charlie was surprised. She'd only ever used spells written down in Agatha's old grimoire.

"Some can," said Agatha. "Not all. Eliza could. At Samhain I'd walk to over to her house. We'd stand together before the old Akelarre, where our sisters had stood for years and years before us. We lit the fire and waited till midnight to see the new year in. We hung our wreaths and we chanted Eliza's spell together in the early hours of the new day, bringing luck and strength to the village to see it through the winter."

Charlie stared at Agatha. She knew where the old Akelarre was – it was the big ancient fireplace in their lounge. Nowadays it had a modern mantelpiece with family photos and a pot plant sitting on it. But still it tingled with the ghost of magic past.

"It's up to you what you put in your wreath," Agatha was saying. "You could put a sigil, like a pentagram…"

Charlie turned to her lever-arch file and found:

Sigils:

    Pentagram
    Pentacle
    Baphomet
    Endless Knot
    All-seeing Eye

"Or you could just use herbs that you like. Focus on what you want for the village in the winter to come. Think about the people, the weather, the crops. Your wreath is personal too, so you can add in a wish for yourself, a goal you want to achieve in the next few months."

Charlie swallowed. She knew what she wanted. She wanted her best friend – her familiar – to be all hers again. She glanced sideways at Kat and turned to her page on herbs. There were herbs for encouraging friendship, for love, but nothing for bonding someone to you.

"I'm just going out to gather some more honeysuckle," said Kat. She closed the cottage door behind her.

"Um," Charlie began quickly, "what herb could I use to link s-s-s-someone to me? I mean, o-o-only to me?"

Agatha put down her wreath and gave Charlie a questioning glance. "Possession?" she said. "That's dark magic, Charlie." She shook her head slightly. "It's wrong to make someone like you or pay attention to you. And even if you bound someone to you by force, it would be meaningless. It is not real if it has to be forced."

Charlie looked away. Her throat was tight.

"I-I have to go," she said. "It's nearly d-d-dinner time. C-can you say goodbye to K-K-Kat for me?"

"OK, Charlie," said Agatha softly. She passed Charlie a twig of honeysuckle. "Hang this over your bed tonight," she said. "I think it'll help."

Glossary of witch terms

Akelarre — a place where witches meet.

Chalk circle (also known as a Ritual circle) — a circle of space to contain energy or protect the spell-caster.

Charm — an item of magic, intended to bring good luck and/or protection to its owner; a spell.

Coven — an association of witches.

Curse — a spell to inflict harm.

Dreamcatcher — a small hoop, often containing feathers and beads, which catches bad dreams or sad thoughts.

Familiar — a creature, usually an animal, with minor magical powers who assists a witch.

Grimoire — a book of spells.

Havoc — a type of bad luck which accompanies

the use of dark magic.

Moon days — witches celebrate four phases of the moon: new moon, waxing moon, full moon and waning moon as well as, less often, a lunar eclipse.

Poppet doll — a figure or doll made to represent a person or animal. Used in spell-craft to focus magic.

Potion — a magical liquid.

Sigil — a symbol of magic such as the star or pentacle.

Sun days — witches celebrate particular days to honour the Sun God, such as Yule, Imbolic, Beltane and the Summer Solstice

Telepathy — the art of communicating with another's mind.

Tincture — oral drops made from herbs.

Witch bottle — a device used to trap or counter a spell or curse.

Items in a Witch's Larder

Apple — encourages balance and harmony, used for healing spells.

Candle wax — use varies according to colour:
White — for purity
Yellow — for creativity
Red — for power
Blue — for harmony
Green - for growth
Orange — for joy

Eggshell — for protection.

Heather — white heather (Erica carnea f. alba) brings luck and protects against evil. Purple heather (calluna vulgaris) assists with spell-casting.

Honey — enhances happiness, helps to bind ingredients together.

Lavender — used to bring peace.

Orange peel — used for happiness spells.

Salt — used for protection and purification spells.

Sandalwood — used for healing and warmth spells.

Sulphur — banishes bad luck.

Useful spells

Good luck spell — to be said at dawn.
Close your eyes and recite:

O rising sun,
On this very day,
I need good luck,
To come my way!

Wish spell — light a candle outdoors at full moon.
Look at the moon for ten seconds, then recite:

By stars above,
By moon, by fire,
Bring to me
My heart's desire!

Friendship spell — make a bracelet from
honeysuckle. Stroke it three times and say:

I open my mind,
I'm ready to start,
New friends I'll find
To soothe my heart!

Abie Longstaff has written many successful picture books, including *The Mummy Shop* and *Just the Job for Dad*, and the Fairytale Hairdresser books. Abie lives in Hove with her family. *How To Trap a Wolf*, the sequel to *How To Catch a Witch*, is publishing in 2017.

SALLY

An Island of Our Own

"A writer of enormous power and strength" *Literary Review*

NICHOLLS